☞ W9-BJQ-683

Templeton, Janet
Love is a scandal

Love Is a Scandal

Love Is a Scandal

JANET TEMPLETON

DOUBLEDAY & COMPANY, INC.

GARDEN CITY, NEW YORK

1984

All of the characters in this book
are fictitious, and any resemblance
to actual persons, living or dead,
is purely coincidental.

Library of Congress Cataloging in Publication Data

Templeton, Janet, 1926-
Love is a scandal.

I. Title.
PS3558.E78L59 1984   813'.54
ISBN: 0-385-19481-1
Library of Congress Catalog Card Number 84-8059

First Edition

For
Ms. Catherine Alexis Hunsburger
and friends

Contents

1. In Which the Reader Is Witness to an Unexpected Meeting
2. Miranda Makes It Clear That She Is Not Her Sister
3. Recriminations Are Evenly Distributed
4. Charlotte Has the Solution
5. Lionel Decides, but Mrs. Saltfield Disposes
6. A Departure Delayed
7. Charlotte Draws a Beau at a Venture
8. A Pearl Before Swains
9. A Bumper Crop in Covent Garden
10. Another Game Is Afoot
11. Two Talks Against Time
12. The Wrong Offer Is Finally Made
13. The Devil to Pay
14. Bad News Is Received and Transmitted
15. A Chapter of Accidents
16. Woman's Wiles
17. Lionel Is Bearded in His Den
18. In Which It Is Shown That Catastrophes Are Ill Timed
19. Faustine Pays a Visit
20. Miranda Pays a Visit
21. An Idea Is Conceived and Lost
22. Journeys End in Lovers' Meetings
23. In Which a Happy Ending Is Produced in Time

Love Is a Scandal

CHAPTER ONE

In Which the Reader Is Witness to an Unexpected Meeting

The comely young girl in the passenger seat of the moving cab was sitting tensely, her slender body leaning forward. She did not look out the windows at views of London which ought to have interested an outlander. The thoughts in her mind were of a different nature, as she busily created difficulties which would evolve in the next days of the new life upon which she was now embarked. Those difficulties would very soon turn into obstacles which would never be surmounted. An existence of eternal tension was what almost any young girl in her situation would have imagined, she felt sure.

Her hired cab suddenly halted with a jarring sound, an incident which gave her ample reason to consider a new worry in the immediate present.

Miranda Powell, for that was the seventeen-year-old female's name, peered out the open window at her left. Ignoring the local manifestations to be seen on this cool September morning in Savile Street, she looked only at the source of the imbroglio before her. No casualties had resulted to human or horse, for which she was grateful. The right front wheel of her cab had somehow locked into a rear wheel of a passing medical brougham of quality, its somber black relieved at mid-carriage by festive yellow. No other festive note appeared in sight.

It was the work of a moment for her cabby to let out a feverish oath and for the brougham's driver to respond in a similar spirit. Each man was soon questioning the other's ancestry and turning the cool air itself blue with various picturesque condemnations.

"Please!" Miranda's voice was small but clear. "Can't you do something about this?"

Her driver nodded, but he took time to wipe his runny nose with the back of a dark glove, then give a slight pull to the scarf that was a badge of office for himself and his colleagues in all weather. Only after he had touched the flat of his topper was protocol fully satisfied, and he descended. The impeccably dressed coachman on the brougham, however, merely murmured something deferential to his passenger and nodded at what he heard before coming down from his perch.

Miranda was left to her own resources in alighting, but managed it swiftly with the grace of youth. She took a moment to smooth down the lilac muslin cloak, which would at least have shown off her bright red hair if a bonnet hadn't been covering her crowning glory. Now that she was on her feet in the City, as London was modestly known, with at least two distaff onlookers in sight, she fully realized what an error she had made in following her sister's advice by coming to the City in 1853 without dressing in the height of fashion. No consolation was offered by the reflection that more than one young girl was afflicted with an envious and married older sister.

She couldn't help feeling more aware of the sibling-inspired faux pas when the passenger of the medical brougham opened the door and surefootedly stepped down.

This was a young man garbed in exactly what was dictated for the male of a good class. A dark coat looked as if it had been grown on him at the same time as the white shirt, small bow tie, plaid trousers, and dark ankle boots. No older than twenty-five, he was dark-haired, with startling deep blue eyes whose irises were nearly as dark as the pupils. He was quite the handsomest man Miranda had ever seen, and she wondered for a moment that her jaw didn't drop in amazement.

"We seem to be in an awkward situation," he said lightly.

Miranda was adept at persiflage in dealing with males, but it crossed her mind immediately that the specimen in front of her must recognize a country mouse by her attire. It was mildly surprising that he would so much as consent to speak with her. The conception of herself being attractive and fresh wasn't one that occurred to her.

"It shouldn't take much longer," he added with a glance at the men straining to disconnect the wheels.

"Indeed I hope not," she found herself saying. That was the resolution she craved. She had previously imagined all sorts of difficulties in her new life, but these had concerned cataclysmic happenings such as fire or a rainfall lasting forty days and nights. Never had her mind conjured up so mundane a circumstance as a mere carriage accident.

"I can almost assure you that it won't be much longer," he responded, glancing to one side for the second or third time.

The profanity and groaning of the two coach drivers could have been clearly heard over to the St. Pancras railway station from which she had come, Miranda supposed. Other vehicles passed back and forth along Savile Street, not halting to offer help. Passersby stopped, but only to chortle at the laboring pair. Back in Kent, able-bodied men would probably have run out from the deeps of the Romney Marshes to offer assistance.

As this young man was apparently courting her good opinion, Miranda asked softly, "Couldn't *you* be of help?"

To his credit, the gentleman didn't look down at the clothes that adorned him by way of indicating that under no circumstances could he consider despoiling them.

"I couldn't do any harm," he admitted, but stayed in place.

Miranda's approval of this male, apart from his undeniable handsomeness, was vanishing quickly. Without any further prod to the imagination, her mind's eye peopled the immediate future with petulant strangers, the ones she would soon be meeting for the first time, and every one of them was complaining bitterly about her having arrived later than expected.

"It is good to know that there are two men on whom a maiden can depend." She was referring, of course, to the cabby and the coachman.

"Yes, indeed," he said in perfect agreement.

She couldn't help raising her head in further disapproval. Any young man in the village of Ryehurst, in Kent, from which she hailed, would have been challenged at having his strength and industriousness put into question. Here, in the City, those qualities were regarded differently, or so it seemed.

"If I were a man I know what *I* would do," she said insistently.

"Perhaps." His smile was amiable, crinkling much of the skin beneath the deep, deep blue eyes. "But would it be necessary?"

"Certainly. I'd go over there and gesture those two men aside, willing workers though they are, and pull the wheels apart by myself."

"That is laudable," he nodded. "After such a spell of exertion, however, I fear you would collapse in the road and have to be hauled away with a hand ambulance, perhaps in sections."

Miranda was incited further by that bantering tone of his. "I would be powerful if I were a man."

"Would you hunt and shoot? Possibly you would play at cricket, belonging to the Zingerees and drawing the stumps at six. If so, the strength you had gained would be of no use in a dilemma such as the one in which we presently find ourselves."

"I would row," she snapped.

He was amused by the quickness and pertinence of her response.

Miranda still had sense enough to appreciate his true courtesy and her own bout of sullen foolishness. At the same time she remained vexed at his failure to help in achieving a solution to the difficulty with which they were confronted.

"If I were a man I wouldn't be a mere adornment," she said, lowering her voice so as not to entertain anyone who might be in earshot. It was the least repayment of his courtesy that could be offered.

As it was, she saw him look away like a man whose sensibilities had been stung, yet who firmly declined to argue about it.

Miranda regretted having spoken so sharply. As it happened, though, there wasn't any time to make even the most brief apology. With a loud *click!* the linked wheels had been disengaged at last.

The coachman and the cabby spoke not a word of congratulations to each other but turned back to their vehicles. The coachman paused in front of his passenger, the young man. A respect-ful cough issued forth from him.

"The matter has been adjusted, my lord," he added.

Miranda's eyes opened wider than nature had normally in-tended. This man was a peer of the realm! She had nearly lost her temper in conversation with a peer of Queen Victoria's realm! Not until now had she known that a full peer could be so young, of an age so close to hers. It gave her hope that perhaps she would meet another one as handsome as he and less in-clined to sound dodgy during what she felt were critical mo-ments.

"May I?" he said softly, at her side.

Miranda realized that he wanted to help her into the cab. It crossed her mind to say that she couldn't bring herself to call upon him to use up all his strength in so complicated a maneu-ver. The words didn't come out, however, and she was grateful for that. He was, after all, offering an olive branch after the minor hostilities on her part that had characterized their meet-ing. Their first and only meeting, she supposed.

His hand appeared below hers. Miranda was aware of strength in him as she raised herself. For a moment they looked into each other's eyes. She felt herself smiling briefly and won-dered if he was smiling in return.

She had to look away long enough to settle herself in the padded seat within, and at that moment he closed the door lightly. As she turned back, he was indeed smiling, his head cocked to one side. Such experience of males as had been granted to Miranda in Ryehurst told her that he wanted to ask who she was and where she might be reached again. He paused, deciding, if she was correct, to act on the impulse.

The pause turned out to be inadvisable. In the split second, Miranda's hired cab got under way, leaving a peer of the realm in the middle of Savile Street. Their first and only encounter was concluding, as it had begun, on a not-quite-satisfactory note.

CHAPTER TWO

Miranda Makes It Clear
That She Is Not Her Sister

Miranda's heart was pounding as she left the hired cab for the last time. In front of her, on a northwest corner along Jermyn Street, was the two-story red brick house in which she would be living from now on until she found a husband or one was discovered for her. This was the house to which she had been summoned by its occupants and the law, both.

The door was answered by a roly-poly butler, whose girth seemed like a symbol for an establishment in which there was a certain liberty to indulge in excess. A good omen, but not one that Miranda was, of course, willing to accept out of hand. Uncertainty nagged at her without any overt reason while an errand boy emerged from the house to help the coachman with her three luggage pieces.

The butler looked around to her right and left, briefly lowering his eyes for a reason she didn't understand at that time.

"Miss Powell? Miss Miranda Powell?" He grinned in welcome rather than merely smiling. "I am Grimm."

He had been ill named, but Miranda supposed she would have been far from the first to make that particular pleasantry.

Miranda followed him into a hall which was distinguished by a polished mahogany table. Paintings had been located upon dark patterned wallpaper and would be illuminated at night by the hanging gas lamps. One of the artworks showed a rosy baby in the arms of a rosy mother. The second was a portrait of the

"Royal ostrich," as Miranda's late father had disrespectfully referred to the Queen's consort, Prince Albert.

A turkey carpet in red distinguished the large sitting room into which Miranda was now led, as did a number of gaseliers and a series of group portraits which seemed in perfect place against light-colored wallpaper. Sundry chairs and couches and elf-sized tables had been placed around the room as well. It might have been comfortable to anyone who was disposed to feel at ease.

Sitting in one of the chairs was a mildly overweight woman with merry eyes and perhaps in her late forties. Her skin was admirably white, and Miranda couldn't tell if it had been glossed over by various powders and liquids such as were considered suitable, from what she understood, for females in the City.

"I am Mrs. Faustine Saltfield," this lady said in a voice that reminded Miranda of a flute in its timbre, without seeming affected. Like Grimm, she looked to Miranda's right and left, eyes down. "But where is your sister?"

"Why, at home!" Miranda couldn't help sounding puzzled. "Where else would a married woman be but with her husband and other connections?"

"I do not understand." Mrs. Saltfield's brows descended in an attempt at fierce concentration. "Is there yet another child of Joseph Powell's? Was he given to letting his wife spawn children with the prodigality of fish?"

"My late father had two children only."

"How can that be? I am to greet a young person named Merle —no, that is not the name. Dear me, I am in such a pother I hardly know names any longer. Miranda is the name. It is Miranda Powell who is to live here."

"I am she."

"That cannot be correct!" Mrs. Saltfield sounded like someone who has suffered a grave offense.

"Ma'am, I am in a position to assure you that I am Miranda Powell."

Faustine Saltfield drew in a deep breath. "You tell me that you

—*you?*—are the younger daughter of Leftenant Joseph Powell of the Army, recently deceased?"

"I do indeed tell you that."

Miranda was uncertain whether or not to be amused. Whatever she had dreaded in the form of obstacles to be encountered over the next days, this incredulity of Mrs. Saltfield's was not among the alternatives. No matter what difficulties one felt equipped to surmount, others for which a person was entirely unprepared would be put in that pilgrim's path. Miranda was coming to accept that formulation of her late father's, stated on several sad occasions, as a truism never to be questioned.

"You—*you?*—are the daughter with whom Joseph—Leftenant Powell of the East Kent 'Buffs,' as the regiment is known— lived when he was not on duty?"

"That is also correct, ma'am."

"I crave to feel absolute certainty in this matter. You are a daughter of that same Leftenant Powell who was killed by a cannon shell accidentally fired in the course of a military exercise?"

"Those are the details as I have heard them, ma'am."

"Truly a man who found himself giving all for England." Mrs. Saltfield had paused to offer a brisk valedictory for the departed officer. Perhaps it crossed her mind that Joseph Powell, with whom she must have been acquainted, would have been wryly amused at passing on in that fashion, considering such remarks as he had often made against government and even royalty.

Mrs. Saltfield looked fully at Miranda for perhaps the first time. She saw a maiden in a skirt too long to be modish and sleeves a half inch too short.

"The red hair is Joseph's," she said reluctantly. "So is the skin coloring. And that chin—no, I could never mistake the chin."

It was that particular feature, jutting out to a greater extent than seemed possible to Miranda's way of thinking, which had always been her greatest physical shortcoming. That it should help to establish her bona fides in this situation in which she had never wanted to find herself seemed only another irony among so many.

Mrs. Saltfield's mind had lighted upon yet another source of wonder, or so it seemed.

"Now I think on it, you must be all of sixteen years old."

"Seventeen, ma'am."

"Why, in that case, Joe—Joseph, I mean—Leftenant Powell must have been forty years old when you were born."

"Forty-two, ma'am."

"A profligate, indeed! A man who never knew when to cease from habits associated with the young!"

Miranda was too startled to take offense. In the same manner as that of the peer she had encountered on Savile Street, she heard herself taking refuge in mild humor such as she had previously scorned.

"If I were younger, ma'am, as you would seem to have preferred, my father would certainly have been older at my birth."

Mrs. Saltfield suddenly threw back her head and laughed. "Certainly that's true! It shows I am fearfully vexed if so simple a point has to be brought to my attention."

Miranda nodded, tentatively returning the first genuine smile that had been offered.

"As I hadn't seen Joseph in many years, I was sure that everything he did in life must have been accomplished at the time of his early youth," Mrs. Saltfield continued thoughtfully. "I can assure you, however, that I felt certain his younger daughter was not yet of an age. That is primarily why I asked my nephew, Wingham, to accept you as his ward. It was a deed to honor a brave gentleman of whom I was at one time very fond and who died for his country as nearly as may be."

Miranda nodded now. One error had led to another, causing her to be sent posthaste to London after a ceremony at law had been hurriedly completed. Until the recent encounter on Savile Street she had been bitter and angry about being made a ward of some distant and probably aged peer. Now, well aware that London could offer marital opportunities unheard of even throughout Kent, Miranda's feelings had changed for the better. She remained nervy, but she was beginning to feel the first stirrings of hope that a better life might lay ahead for her.

"It is unfortunate," Mrs. Saltfield added, "that I was unable to visit you at your former home and that Wingham couldn't make the time."

Miranda agreed silently, remembering that she had been sullen and angry about not having seen those people who had decided that she must lodge in the far-off home they shared. As an expression of that anger, she had accepted her sister's suggestion about dressing out of fashion during the hegira to the City, and she had been regretting it since those first moments on Savile Street and the sight of that handsome stranger's deep blue eyes.

"I'm sorry to say that neither Lionel nor I, my dear, ever looked at the papers that were formally submitted in Chancery to make Lionel's guardianship a finality." Having verbally flogged herself to her satisfaction, Mrs. Saltfield shrugged massively. "Nothing will now be done about those omissions as they cannot be called back. But I feel free to admit that I do not know what *is* to be done, now."

"Done about what, ma'am?"

"Why, the simple but immutable fact that you are of an age and that Lionel, my nephew, the Earl of Wingham, is only slightly older and is not yet wed. Further, you and he are to be living here, under this roof."

For the first time, Miranda fully comprehended the reasons for Mrs. Saltfield's distress. The woman's point was well-taken and sensible in these circumstances. True, she also lived here, as her attitude had made plain, but the notion of a young man and a female ward of a likely age being so close would be perfect fodder for gossip. The Earl of Wingham's reputation would be punctured if not mortally wounded, and Miranda's opportunities for a good marriage might well be shattered on the same day as they had arisen.

Mrs. Saltfield saw that Miranda looked stricken and reacted as older persons have been doing from time immemorial.

"Some food will get your mind off these things for a while at least," she decided, smiling in a kindly way at Miranda's distress. "Come with me."

A saddened Miranda followed out of the sitting room to a chamber just off the kitchen. Here, in a welter of paintings and statues, gewgaws on small tables, and large doll miniatures of children and dogs, was a square table with four chairs. Very likely this particular branch of the British Museum was used for informal feedings.

Had Miranda been less bemused, she would have heard some withering exchanges of conversation between Mrs. Saltfield and the cook. The latter, who had prepared hokeypokey for a young arrival, was appalled that food for adults was to be served instead, as the Earl's ward was a full seventeen years old.

Miranda did happen to hear and look up as a parlormaid gasped at first sight of her. It seemed likely that by now there was already sufficient material for the beginnings of a juicy scandal.

She addressed herself dutifully to the veal with a side dish of sea kale but didn't forget the dilemma that had been visited upon her as well as the others. Mrs. Saltfield, having wanted to tell a few stories about her late friend, Joseph Powell, found herself stopped by the pained look that persisted on the girl's features.

Miranda's mind was flirting with the thought of running off and perhaps even of starving to death in a ditch while she tried to beg the railway fare back to Kent. Regretfully, for it was an agreeable life that she saw being truncated, she finished the last dollop of sea kale and then wondered if she might not borrow a carriage in which to be driven back to Ryehurst in grand style.

Mrs. Saltfield, too, had been considering the awesome Gordian knot. "A talk with Lionel will certainly be required before any decision whatever can be made about this matter."

"The Earl?" Miranda finished the last of her oolong and looked up. "Yes, where is he, then?"

"He has had to leave the house suddenly for an hour, perhaps."

Miranda pursed her lips. She had imagined no one but herself being delayed. Now it seemed beyond doubt that miscalculations could occur to others, could happen to residents of the City as well as to emigrants like herself. She felt slightly more at ease.

The brief respite from unsettled feelings lasted till shortly after both females had returned to the large sitting room. There was the sound of a man's footsteps in the hall, and then this door opened and a voice she was sure she had heard for the first time not long ago was calling out cheerfully.

"Where is the little one?"

At that moment she gasped.

He turned, raising his head.

Miranda could feel his eyes upon her, those unforgettable deep blue eyes with the irises almost as dark as the pupils.

CHAPTER THREE

Recriminations Are Evenly Distributed

"I do not believe this," said Lionel, the Earl of Wingham, after the briefest of possible pauses.

There was an amused glint in those distinctively colored eyes. It was worth noting to his credit that at the same time as he could unquestionably visualize awkwardness ahead he managed to find some wry amusement at the *bizarrerie* of this second encounter.

Miranda had regained her calm after the realization of her guardian's persona. Within her breast was the sudden feeling of a type of pleasure which was new to her. The knowledge of impending closeness to a handsome and generous peer whose age couldn't be far greater than her own was a prospect that she found happily exciting.

Mrs. Saltfield, in an even higher voice than usual, said, "This —this is your ward, Miranda by name."

"How do you do?"

Miranda stood, then curtsied politely. She didn't know whether or not to wink by way of indicating that she recalled him, but decided against that. He might come to the conclusion that she was being forward instead of only expressing happiness.

The Earl couldn't bring himself to make the acknowledgment of her unexpected presence.

"I am grateful to be the object of your benevolence," Miranda continued sweetly. "In time I hope to make you proud of me."

"I see." He had started to smile, but the seriousness of this new development made him halt. "Aunt Faustine, we must have a discussion."

Miranda hadn't anticipated, somehow, that a conversation about her presence would take place between the two adults only. She could imagine solutions involving violence being bruited about in order to eliminate the embarrassment, as they might have considered her. For once she knew that she was being overly imaginative, like a child whose presence the others had been expecting. She shook her head quickly and remained silent.

"Aunt Faustine, have Grimm or one of the maids take Miss Powell up to her room and wait until she is sent for."

No word from him directly to her was going to be spoken. Miranda brought herself to look away from the Earl only when a maid appeared and led her out. No remark had been made about her unfashionable garb, such as she had dreaded, presumably because both adults had been concerned with different matters.

She was led up a carpeted staircase and into a narrow hall with hunting scenes framed on the blood-red wallpaper. To appreciate hunting, apparently, one had to live in London.

Miranda's room was the farthest from the staircase on the second floor. She took a couple of steps in and then halted, her jaw dropping.

It was an airy enough room with yellow wallpaper displaying drawings of animals consorting with others of their kind in the greatest of amity. Paintings of serene young girls and friendly-looking nannies decorated the walls at suitable intervals, or perhaps the older women were parents. Tables contained various dolls representing animals and young girls, all intended for play by somebody far younger than Miranda. Bookshelves sported some dozen issues of *The Girl's Own Paper,* along with such volumes as *Famous Girls.* When the tenant presumably wanted more adult fare, if ever, she could reach out for *Twelve Notable Good Women,* by Rosa N. Carey. It wasn't at all as ghastly as an accommodation at the Chateau D'If, for instance, but the room prepared for Miranda would have perfectly suited a mere child. She was too old for her room.

At some time in the past, she might have sobbed bitterly in hopeless frustration, but the surroundings of this chamber and her reactions to them made her realize that she was no longer mentally fit for the responses of childhood. It could be that the day's trials had helped her grow some other way than in height.

The Right Honorable Earl of Wingham paced his large sitting room almost as if it were the enclosure at Goodwood racetrack. He kept both hands behind him and pressed against the plaid trousers as if for dear life and to somehow aid his efforts in getting a perspective on the situation in which he found himself.

He wasn't a man given to displays of temper and actually showed a tendency to shrug off the sort of difficulties that caused others to curse like navvies. But he knew a classic imbroglio when, so to speak, it reared its head.

Aunt Faustine was saying hurriedly, "My dear Lionel, I simply had no idea in the world that Miranda was so mature. Even for her age she looks distinctly mature."

"It's beside the point that you didn't know." The Earl suddenly thrust both hands into the pockets of his lounge coat. "How am I going to straighten it out? *That* is to the point at this juncture."

In all truth the girl's attractiveness was by no means unimportant. He was well aware of her considerable charms, just as he had been aware of them at the brief meeting in Savile Street. There was no apparent need of mentioning this latter incident to Aunt Faustine and distracting that good lady still further. Under no circumstances, however, did he want Miss Powell living under his roof.

"Even if there was no other reason to surgically excise that girl from our home, there is the consideration that her presence might imperil a distinct upward step in my career." He had expected to be giving this news with joy but sounded bitterly amused instead. "George Hamilton Gordon, the Fourth Earl of Aberdeen and First Minister to Queen Victoria, has asked me to join the Elgin Commission in negotiating a treaty with the United States in the matter of trading with Canada."

"That's wonderful," Mrs. Saltfield started. "It's what you've always wanted, Lionel, a foothold in the diplomatic community of nations. I'm so pleased for you."

"Thank you, my dear aunt." He smiled, but only briefly. The Great Imbroglio had once again bobbed to the surface of his mind. "But can you imagine what people will be saying now as soon as everything becomes known? There will be a scandal which can destroy my career in diplomacy before it has properly begun."

Mrs. Saltfield tried in vain not to parade her own distress. She had looked forward to long conversations with Miranda Powell on the subject of her late father. Indeed, Joseph Powell had been the only man she ever loved and the only one she had wanted to marry. More was the pity that her late mother had insisted she plight her troth instead with the wealthy Reginald Saltfield, now deceased. She had become fond of Reginald over the childless years in the same way that one develops a likeness for some neighbor's bulldog.

In hopes of retaining one little pleasure to help tide her over the coming winter, Mrs. Saltfield made the strenuous effort to find a modus vivendi for the three of them under one roof.

"Can't we say that Miranda is on a visit?"

"Everybody in society and many in government are well aware that I have taken a ward."

"And certainly no harm is intended."

On this point Lionel found himself disconcertingly sensitive.

"Of course no wickedness is intended," he said, making what he didn't think of as a subtle distinction and raising his voice while he was at it. "But you can imagine as well as I can exactly what it is that important people are going to say when it becomes a matter of common knowledge that I now have custody of a nubile maiden."

"Not everyone will think the worst of you. Evil to him who evil thinks, as the French say. But they speak in French, of course," she added, making it clear that not even the brazen French would venture upon witty remarks while using the Queen's English.

"I am disturbed because of what the nice nellies in

Aberdeen's cabinet will say." Lionel paced the room, partly disarranging his well-combed dark hair. "The law says that I am in control of my ward's education, and there will be sniggers about what I'm doing in order to educate her."

"Lionel!"

"And let me point out that the laws of Chancery also give me the right to the enjoyment of my ward's services. The exact words. Can you imagine how that conception will be twisted around by some of those evil minds?"

"I am beyond blushing." But his insistence had called realism to the fore. Mrs. Saltfield faced the knowledge that men, like frail womankind, were lured by gossip and scandal. "However, there is some foundation to your imaginings, Lionel. I feel bound to concur in that much."

"All I can see for it is for my solicitors to petition the Queen to become Miranda Powell's guardian at Chancery." The Earl suddenly shook his head. "No. That, I am certain, on second thought, can only be done under the laws against cruelty to children."

He didn't have to add that such a petition must cause a scandal in itself. As for his role on the Elgin Commission and a career in the diplomatic service, it would be nonexistent from that moment onward. In Good Queen Victoria's Golden Days there could be scandals within scandals.

"I see only one course to follow," the Earl insisted. "No one outside the house, no one whatever, must know about what has happened."

"It is an unexceptionable desire," Mrs. Saltfield agreed. "How are you to make certain that no one discovers the truth?"

At this moment of all times there was an interruption. Grimm, that cheery butler whose demeanor belied his name, entered.

"A visitor has arrived."

Too many seismic disturbances are considered injurious to the equilibrium. Lionel Formond, the Second Earl of Wingham, felt as if he had withstood a rainstorm only to find himself in the midst of some tropical earthquake.

"Are you sure?" he asked, and then shook his head and

regained control of himself immediately. He didn't condone
asking senseless questions. "Well, then, who is it?"

"Miss Dempster, Your Lordship."

Charlotte Dempster was the attractive and admirable
maiden to whom the Earl had been engaged over the past year.
In his current state he found no cause to wonder why he had not
considered her during these last minutes.

"Ask her to wait," he instructed urgently, wanting time to
pull himself together.

It was already too late. Charlotte Dempster had entered the
room moments behind Grimm, one hand waving a package
that Lionel felt certain was intended for a youngster. She was
looking at a point only slightly above the turkey carpet.

"Where is the little tyke?" Charlotte asked sunnily. "It would
be too cruel of you, Lionel dear, to keep me from seeing her
immediately."

CHAPTER FOUR

Charlotte Has the Solution

In the course of an account that is studded with so much despair and *Sturm und Drang,* with turmoil and soul-searching so convulsive as to make the great Russian novelists look to their laurels, a few words have to be interpolated in offering an introduction to Miss Charlotte Dempster.

It is Miss Dempster who will appear to be thwarting others in their pursuit of such laudable goals as eternal happiness and prodigious wealth. Arriving at a quick and unfavorable conclusion about her character is to do her a grievous injustice. She was a kindly young woman of not more than twenty summers, a childhood friend of an astute Lionel with no patience for the meanness of others, and the daughter of almost impoverished parents with whose interests she was properly concerned. None could be found in the length and breadth of the City to speak a bad word about Charlotte Dempster, and it is this truth which must be borne in mind during the narrative which follows.

In appearance she was middle-sized, with bright yellow hair and mocking gray eyes. Her figure was splendidly displaying a lace bodice crinoline in azure from the Farmer and Rogers emporium on Regent Street. A purist, searching rigorously for some major blemish in her aspect, would have to retire from the lists and confess abject defeat.

"Where is little Miranda?" Miss Dempster asked in the musical voice that was one of her most charming attributes.

"She's very tired," Lionel lied promptly, offering a warm smile that was genuine. He almost always felt at ease in Charlotte's presence. "She has gone up to sleep."

"When may I see her, Lionel dear? As we're all to be living together after the marriage, then the sooner I make her acquaintance, the better."

"Of course, yes." Practice in deception was giving Lionel an aura of confidence. "Tomorrow afternoon I am certain that she will be ready for you."

"I hope that little Miranda isn't going to be frightened at the strangeness of everything in her new life. Should I see her before then, I could offer some comfort."

"Come by in the morning, if you insist."

"A hearty welcome indeed." It crossed her mind that dear Lionel was under some stress, but she attributed this to obstacles in pursuit of his true vocation as a diplomat.

"I didn't mean—" He stopped himself and smiled yet again. He would have told Charlotte exactly what was wrong, but he felt that she would be embarrassed at having brought such an inappropriate gift. He was certainly fond enough of Charlotte so that he didn't want to cause any such feelings in her.

"Leave that gift of yours, and you can trot it out tomorrow."

"Grimm can put it away," she agreed.

Lionel escorted her out. In the hallway, not far from the portrait of Prince Albert which had prompted Miranda's scorn, Charlotte paused. The carpeted staircase leading upstairs was at her left hand.

"I could slip up there and see her asleep," Charlotte said softly, eyes glowing. "Children always throw off their coverings, and I can put little Miranda's back in place."

"I appreciate your interest, but I wish we could postpone your meeting with Miranda until tomorrow in the morning." It crossed his mind that by seeing Charlotte tonight, as he planned to do, it would be possible to reveal the truth at last. She might evolve a stratagem for dealing with the possible repercussions of his foray into guardianship. At the least she'd find a chuckle for him over the position in which he discovered himself.

Alert though he may have been, he was not prepared for the happenings of the next minute.

Charlotte, having looked toward the carpeted stairs she had

wanted to ascend in order to meet the little girl, suddenly called out with surprise.

Lionel's eyes followed hers. His heart sinking, he understood what had brought on the unseemly emotional display. At a bend in the dark staircase he, like Charlotte, could see an elongated shadow.

It was, of course, Miranda who was causing the shadow to fall. She had come out of her room, attracted by the sight through her window of a large-sized carriage and wanting to see what sort of person would be riding in it to visit the house in which she was now living. Miranda didn't have experience enough to know that the particular carriage wasn't a symbol of affluence, and couldn't possibly have been aware that Charlotte's parents occasionally borrowed it from a baron who remembered them kindly from their richer days.

Miranda did know, however, that she had been observed. She assumed that her features must of course be plain to the attractive woman on the lower level. She took several more steps down, ready to flee at the slightest sign of disapproval. Sudden resolution was raised in her by the Earl's stunned silence and her desire to prove that he didn't necessarily have to be ashamed of a country mouse like herself. Miranda was almost walking firmly when she reached the lowest step.

"You are the ward?" this woman asked after a pause, but in notably pleasant tones. Unlike Mrs. Saltfield, she didn't repeat pronouns with undisguised incredulity. "Miranda?"

"Yes. Yes, I am."

Miranda was still trying terribly hard to be sophisticated but she was being unsettled. Her eyes darted from side to side as if searching for an escape, and she licked her lips nervously.

Charlotte, observing the young girl's reactions, couldn't help feeling sympathetic. She was well aware that dear Lionel had for once tampered with the truth in talking to her just now and indeed that the presence in Jermyn Street of so mature a female unrelated by blood ties to Lionel or herself was bound to cause rumors of a sort unmentionable in public as a rule. All the same, the poor girl was clearly a prey to uncertainty, and Charlotte responded with typical warmth.

Softly but sincerely she said, "Welcome to London, Miranda."

"Thank you very much, miss."

"My name is Charlotte."

"Thank you very much, miss—Charlotte, I mean."

Miranda's shy smile was enough to light up her features and put a gleam into the wide, forest-green eyes. She thought she heard the Earl suddenly draw in his breath but wasn't sure.

Charlotte had been unaware of any manifestation along that line but did observe Miranda's great attractiveness. Like almost everyone else who ever saw a self-possessed Miranda, even for moments, Charlotte found herself charmed.

"And now you will have to pardon me," Charlotte said, offering a regretful smile of her own. She moved off, not wanting for once to be near her affianced because of this first mendaciousness she had ever encountered in him. Head high, she strode firmly out to her waiting carriage.

Lionel knew more about women than to follow one of the species and try to make explanations when she was in her first full flush of irritation. At night he would see Charlotte, and there was certain to be time for some reasonable discussion, as he had previously felt, and an exploration of possibilities.

He grinned up at Miranda Powell, having decided that there was no necessity for causing her any continuing unease. Nothing that had taken place here was the fault of this lovely child, as he now thought of her. This unfortunate child.

"I'll ask Mrs. Saltfield, my aunt, to take you for some more stylish clothes when she has the time for a shopping expedition," he said agreeably.

It was a prospect to which she would ordinarily have looked forward with glee, but she recollected her older sister claiming that girls in the City had to dress in some uncivilized mode which couldn't be described to a Kentish miss. It took a moment before she told herself firmly that her older sister had been lying on account of jealousy caused by the notion of Miranda having a great adventure.

By that time Lionel had decided that for some reason yet another inducement to draw a smile was necessary.

"I'll have you put into a different room, if you like, or have some of the childish gewgaws taken out of the room you've been given."

"Thank you, Your Lordship."

Miranda did smile this time. During the last thirty minutes she had discovered a drawing on the wallpaper that showed a frog in spectacles and reading from the Good Book to a number of well-behaved younger frogs. That illustration, instead of being a comfort to the imaginative Miranda, seemed a conception of unmitigated horror.

"I'll leave you to your own devices now," he said, contentedly finishing the second discussion between them. "Feel free to inspect the premises if you like, but avoid my study. You'll recognize it from the outside as the closed double door at the end of the ell."

He was on his way to spend a few hours by himself. What with this full day of happenings he felt the overpowering need to take some deep breaths in familiar surroundings where he wouldn't be interrupted.

The party which Lionel and his aunt were to attend was taking place at Gray's Inn. A library of law volumes was the backdrop for the reception, which was to be followed in another room with a concert being offered by two aspiring brides. The affair, given by the Baron and Lady Passy, was intended to celebrate their only son's having been called to the bar at last. The number of failed previous attempts by their scion had made the candidate a legend in his own circles and others. During the struggle to become a proctor and show his skills in Admiralty Court, he had fathered six children, four of them within marriage. One of those boys would shortly be coming down from Cambridge.

From the moment Lionel entered by the High Holborn entrance, courteously deferring to his aunt as the cloaks were stowed away, he was searching for Charlotte. It distracted him that the swallow-tailed evening coat he was wearing for the first time should draw approval from everyone he knew as well as a host of strangers who had never seen such an article of wearing apparel.

After he offered his greetings to the host and hostess along with congratulations to their offspring, the Honorable Victor, a title that had led to much derisive comment in the past, Lionel resumed his knightly quest for his affianced's whereabouts.

Interruptions continued to come from all sides, or so it seemed. The bald and bearded Marquess of Salisbury offered congratulations on the newly styled garment. Mr. John Bright stated his dislike of it in the form of a speech. Lord Palmerston silently approved the coat. Mr. Disraeli, the dandified Tory, tactfully ignored the coat and praised the kid leg-lace boots Lionel was wearing, also for the first time. Congratulations on his appointment to the Elgin Commission were only briefly interspersed between sartorial observations of pith and eloquence.

Mr. Augustus Egg, the painter, suggested that a portrait of Lionel might be useful. Mr. John Thadeus Delane, the editor of the *Times*, looked appraisingly at Lionel but said nothing worth repeating. Lionel was pleased to find himself in conversation with a Miss Mary Ann Evans, who had been introduced to him as a novelist. These pourparlers gave him no time to look covertly around the library, as he had hoped on finding himself with one of the fair sex. His aunt interrupted to acquaint him with the apple-cheeked Dr. William Palmer of Rugely in Staffordshire, adding that so pleasant-mannered a medical man would have found a splendid future if he practiced in the City.

Charlotte was in the smaller room, standing between her parents. A rose merino dress with the lowest decent neckline emphasized the whiteness of her skin along with other charms, and the center part in her blond hair gave an impression of serenity belied by her narrowed eyes and the too-wide smile Lionel remembered unfavorably from their childhood years.

He heard himself greeted temperately, but without enthusiasm. After acknowledging in kind, he spoke to the Dempsters. They were among the present company because their host and hostess remembered them kindly from the days before Mr. Dempster's various investments had combined to nearly impoverish that worthy gentleman.

Charlotte had moved slightly out of their hearing while he

was involved with her elders, and now he joined her for the
second time.

"I was too concerned with other matters to give you the news
immediately," he began, hoping that her pleasure at hearing it
was going to curtail any distress she might feel about the other
matter, as he thought of it. "I have been offered a post on the
Elgin Commission and will, of course, accept."

Charlotte's face glowed. "How wonderful for you!" As if
aware that she had been civilized rather than icy to him over
the recent breach of manners, she looked away.

He said quickly, "You mustn't be angry because of my not
having introduced you to Miranda back at Jermyn Street. Coming on top of the Elgin Commission matter, I was unsettled at
seeing the child for the first time."

"Miranda Powell is not a child!"

"The young lady, then. I don't think we have to discuss niceties of language at a time like this."

"You have catapulted yourself into a domestic situation rife
with possibilities for scandal," Charlotte pointed out needlessly.
"It would be possible for you to become another Duke of Barnwell."

Lionel agreed silently. The Duke's behavior with a certain
class of women had lost him a membership at the exclusive
Carlton Club and exposed him to obloquy at the United University and United Whist clubs as well. His status was even imperiled at the Harwich Yachting, where the membership commit-
tee was known to accept Viscounts and Honorables.

"I feel certain," Lionel said calmly, "that your confidence in
me will be enough to destroy any foul rumors before birth."

"Can you believe that? Rumors are passed around always and
hurt careers and social lives with abandon. I can think of half a
dozen examples in which the condemnation was wholly unde-
served, but great damage was accomplished all the same."

Lionel could have added several others involving civil servants as well as peers. He grimaced.

"If you have suggestions," he said, "prepare to make them
now."

"Only one possibility occurs to me, much as I dislike it,"

Charlotte said gloomily. "It is most uncharitable, and I am not usually that sort of person."

"Agreed. Surely you aren't suggesting that I hang the young woman as a means of expressing my disapproval of her."

"This is not an occasion for levity," Charlotte remarked. "Miranda is a young girl and most attractive, a girl who has been raised in some province or other and has come to London with the confident anticipation of beginning a new life. At the very least, she ought to experience a London season. Many a peer would be dazzled by her freshness."

"Yes, I'm sure."

"But if she has a season, being your ward, and further a ward who lives under one roof with you, Lionel, you will in turn be exposed to such contumely that the Duke of Barnwell is going to be characterized as a saint in comparison."

"Then you feel that Miranda should not remain in the City."

"She *must not* remain!"

"I do take your meaning."

"Lionel dear, I will state the matter in such terms as to put it beyond further disputation. For the sake of your career and future, as well as our impending marriage, Miranda Powell must be sent away."

Lionel knew persuasive reasoning when he heard it. Reluctantly he nodded.

"I cannot send her back to Kent," he said. "Her friends would disparage her and any chance for a local marriage might be imperiled. But I do think that a boarding school for young ladies would suit the purpose, a school that isn't so far that I can't occasionally visit."

Charlotte looked surprised.

"As guardian of young Miranda's welfare, I have to be in a position to make certain that all is well with her. I do have a court-appointed responsibility."

"The further she is sent off, the better, I would think. However, I leave that to you." She touched him urgently on a sleeve. "But for all our sakes (except hers, as I am sorry to say once more) she should be out of the Jermyn Street house before a rumor about you can gain the slightest footing. She should have left by sundown tomorrow at the latest."

It seemed a short time indeed, but again common sense was on her side.

"I suppose you're right." He couldn't help wondering with what words he could inform the lovely Miranda about this reversal of her fortunes. "You're certainly right."

CHAPTER FIVE

Lionel Decides, but Mrs. Saltfield Disposes

Miranda awoke with a feeling of pleased anticipation that it took moments to identify. She had apparently recollected as soon as her eyes were open that a shopping expedition was to be undertaken on this day. The objective would be to dress her in the latest of fashions as currently worn by London society females. It was an objective of which she fully approved.

Although she was to be freshly outfitted, she was determined to enter a dressmaker's establishment clothed so respectably that no modiste would look askance at her. As a result she chose a day dress in the shade she referred to as cucumber green, not a color she especially liked but one which gave her the look of propriety, which was always persuasive.

In the hall she paused only to seal her eternal friendship with the affectionate bulldog of the establishment, a brown-eyed hound named Pam, after the well-known nickname of Henry Temple, the Third Viscount Palmerston. Separating herself with difficulty from Pam's enfolding clutches, she hurried down at long last, looking eagerly to her right and left.

The large sitting room beckoned because her companion in shopping was seated there. Forgoing breakfast if only for a while, Miranda hurried inside.

"I will be ready as soon as I have demolished a kipper or two," she said cheerily. "Or I can postpone eating at all until the day's ructions are completed."

"Oh, have your breakfast by all means." Mrs. Saltfield, although seated and with hands on the arms of her chair, looked as if she was prepared to fall into the turkey carpet and lose herself. The normally fluting voice had been lowered, not quite to the level of basso profundo but certainly far from its usual perky reaches.

"Are you ill?" Miranda asked, justifiably concerned.

"In a way, yes." Mrs. Saltfield's lips were pursed bitterly at the corners. "There will be no shopping."

"That is perfectly understandable in the circumstances," Miranda said promptly, even though it seemed that such regrets ought to have been her own response. "Permit me to call for help."

"No, that isn't going to be necessary, but I thank you for the good offices."

Mrs. Saltfield now sighed in a multinote fashion that could probably have been transcribed and entered at Stationers Hall to be copyrighted as a dirge. Ever since Lionel had spoken to her in the carriage on the way back from the Passys' gruesome entertainment last night, she had been most unhappy. Truly the good woman had looked forward to expending part of the oncoming winter in discussions with this young female about the only man she had ever loved. Now it was not to be. The hardwon pleasure had been snatched away by Lionel after prodding from Charlotte. No doubt Miss Dempster had put in some well-chosen words about prudence and its place in the scheme of things. Until then, Mrs. Saltfield had always been unreservedly fond of Charlotte, but that opinion was in the process of being revised to some extent.

She was aware that Miranda was showing a very real concern for an older woman's well-being. The knowledge caused her to speak rather than keen.

"Wingham has decided that new clothes won't actually be necessary for you back in Kent."

"But I don't understand!" Miranda's eyes opened wide. "What *can* you mean?"

"Only that you are being returned to your village," Mrs. Saltfield said bitterly. "Like a package that is not accepted from the post, you are being returned."

Miranda's first thought, so unprepared was she for the announcement, was simply that a lively imagination such as hers didn't offer the least protection against the slings and arrows of outrageous guardians. Having amused herself, however briefly, she realized that the matter was not only serious but crushing.

In the past, as part of what she now considered her youth, Miranda had always been fully prepared to burst into tears at the slightest provocation and insist that the end of the world had arrived for her. Now, given what she rightly felt was a major setback in her life, she did nothing more than to stiffen her back and regret that she would never again be able to indulge herself in a full-fledged tantrum.

A moment's anger did show itself, she was sure. Never had Miranda seriously considered that she was an object of anyone's charity or compassion. The Earl of Wingham was treating her like some lad from a Blue-Coat school who was levels beneath him in society and a possible drain on his feelings.

"I can assure you," Mrs. Saltfield added, "that even when the Earl is married to Miss Dempster, to whom he is engaged and whom he has known from childhood, he will continue to take an interest in your affairs. You remain a member of the family."

"A distant relation, so to say."

"Yes. Yes, I fear so."

Miranda couldn't help being surprised that the Earl would choose to plight his troth with some girl known to him from childhood. She tried to imagine herself marrying one of the boys with whom she had been acquainted from the cradle or a little afterwards and shuddered at the prospect. In such a relationship there could be no delight, no surprise, no ecstasy. It was like choosing to wear the same clothing for one's natural life.

Such a decision was Wingham's concern, however. Miranda still felt herself powerfully drawn to his lordship, but her feelings mattered not at all.

Mrs. Saltfield, her eyes taking in the turkey carpet as if it had offended her, added quietly, "I will send the housekeeper—have you met her? Mrs. Jossy—upstairs to pack for you."

"I thank you, but it will be unnecessary to distract that lady from her other duties," Miranda said proudly. "My effects were not yet wholly unpacked, and it will cause no difficulty whatever to make the slight change."

Mrs. Saltfield offered no response, well aware that she and Wingham and the house and even the surrounding city had been sadly but decidedly rebuked.

"I bid you a good morning," said Miranda, taking some of the sting out of her tone; after all, what had happened couldn't have been foreseen by this lonely woman. "I hope to speak with you again before taking my leave of this house and its denizens."

Mrs. Saltfield, left to her own devices, stood determinedly and raised her crinoline with a hand. Then she started out to the alcove, where she had previously agreed to issue a report about the proceedings which had just concluded so painfully.

She was angry, only in part because her intention to help in raising Joseph Powell's younger child had been thwarted by understandable circumstances. But it was apparent to her that a girl so bright and gallant, so warm and fresh, ought to spend at least one season in the City. Miranda Powell could receive an offer, as a result, from one of a covey of wealthy and perhaps even titled young men. Permitting nature to take its course, Mrs. Saltfield would have helped accomplish a good deed in memory of the one man she had ever loved, in memory of Joseph.

As a result of these musings, it was a determined Faustine Saltfield who rushed out to that miniature museum which had been installed in the alcove. She had expected to find Lionel and did, his distressed features almost the whey coloring of his corded woollen trousers and jacket. Seated at the table, in a rose day dress with dark puffed sleeves, was none other than Charlotte Dempster. Charlotte had probably hurried over to make sure that the deed was done quickly. It was no surprise to Mrs. Saltfield, disturbed as she herself felt, to see the concern—almost certainly for Miranda Powell's feelings—clearly etched on the young woman's attractive features.

"It is done," Mrs. Saltfield announced.

Charlotte asked promptly, "Does the girl need comforting?"

Faustine Saltfield was taken aback, in spite of herself, at being in the presence of a benevolent Lady Macbeth, who urged others to perform nefarious actions and then made great efforts to minimize the consequences. It wasn't really to be wondered at, however. The generous Charlotte had been encumbered with improvident parents who needed financial care such as would result in the wake of that marriage of which she was eventually going to be a part.

Mrs. Saltfield wanted to make her plea directly, but the urgency which drove Charlotte Dempster would keep that young woman from making a favorable response. And it was clear, too, that Charlotte would be agonized as a result because she was plainly hurting another human being. No alternative remained for Faustine Saltfield but to adopt that ruse upon which she swiftly decided as she looked from one agitated set of features to the other.

"What Miranda Powell needs," said Mrs. Saltfield, drawing herself up, "is a talking-to."

Charlotte, misunderstanding, rose to her feet. "I shall go up immediately and do my best to offer explanations and apologies."

"That was not my meaning." As each female's voice was notable for its speaking range, Mrs. Saltfield and Charlotte sounded as if they were in the throes of some musical duet from the facile pen of Signor Verdi. "A rating by someone forbidding of aspect is required in that girl's case."

"What do you mean, Aunt?" Lionel, who had not been able to speak until now, whirled on her. He had been pacing the alcove, hands crossed behind his back.

"Someone must strictly tell Miranda Powell to always repeat to others the full and complete reasons for what has taken place, for your taking the action upon which you have insisted."

"I am sure Miranda will do so without having to be rated," Charlotte said, seeing the best side of the situation. "If you, Mrs. Saltfield, have told her about my being engaged to Lionel, dear Lionel, then there can be no need to strike terror into Miss Powell's heart. She can use her mother wit to deduce the reasons for dear Lionel's proper behavior."

"I did indeed tell her about my nephew's forthcoming marital status, but something must be done all the same and done before she leaves. You clearly fail to perceive the likely alternative."

"I do indeed," Charlotte conceded.

"I fear that instead of giving the complete reasons behind what has taken place, Miranda, from motives of wanting to bypass the recounting in full of a difficult experience, may offer merely the bare facts." Startled at having referred to nudity in any form whatever, Mrs. Saltfield hurried on. "Miranda has only to say that her guardian insisted upon this unfavorable outcome, and local tongues will be wagging at a ferocious rate."

"But why should they?"

"Can neither of you visualize what may happen if the girl hasn't been clear as crystal in her explanations at all times? Some native on the heath or the marsh, or whatever it may be that disfigures the terrain in Kent, will pretend to be worldly and offer an odious speculation as undiluted fact."

Charlotte's lips formed an O of surprise and understanding.

Having already used her vocal chords to discuss a forbidden topic in mixed company, Mrs. Saltfield found her second venture of that type coming more easily. "Some fool has only to say that Miranda was forced to submit to her guardian's loathsome caresses and was sent home as a result rather than be permitted to complain to others in the City."

Lionel looked momentarily bemused, rather than indulging in debate about the nature and quality of such caresses as he might ever in life have bestowed upon those of the fair sex.

Mrs. Saltfield's attention was riveted by the brisk play of emotions on his face. She couldn't help feeling that she had gained a measure of revenge upon her nephew for his having shocked her by referring to lustful excesses during their first conversation about Miranda Powell and her impact on the two of them.

"Gossip and rumor," Charlotte said, turning to her affianced in distress. "Our lives are being plagued by the possibility, Lionel dear, not only in London but as far away as Kent, too."

"Let us be calm, Charlotte." Determined to make one statement upon which everyone could agree, he hesitated. The possibility did indeed exist that his burgeoning career in public service could be damaged by such a chapter of accidents as his aunt had described.

He finally said, "It doesn't matter a fig whether or not the girl is addressed in a critical manner while she is on these premises. The moment she leaves Jermyn Street, she is away from my sphere of influence, from my control (such as that might be), entirely."

Mrs. Saltfield used the voice of a woman deeply concerned. "What, then, is to be done?"

Lionel had already evolved the answer she desired, as seemed likely with a man of his mental prowess and his capacity to find solutions to knotty brangles.

"If I am to be hanged for doing something and also hanged if I do nothing," he said swiftly, validating his aunt's conclusion, "it is better to do something."

"You are not going to bully—"

Charlotte was prepared to defend the honor of womanhood against verbal assault by the rapacious male.

"I am not."

"If you do intend to bully that child," she said firmly, forgetting how vehemently she had denied in the past that Miranda Powell was in the first flush of youth, "then I will insist upon sternly overseeing your actions."

"I don't plan to be anything but commonsensical," Lionel insisted.

"How can you accomplish that without at least threatening to use *force majeure* upon the child?"

"Follow a few paces behind me and don't speak for a while. All will then be made plain to you, I promise."

CHAPTER SIX

A Departure Delayed

Miranda was concluding preparations for a departure in the same mood as that in which she had first ventured on this expedition. She had changed back into the violet merino dress, which showed off her flaming red hair but was out of the London style because of the diagonal frills. This she covered with that unfashionable lilac cloak which she had also worn upon arrival. She would be leaving this luxury-laden Gehenna in the same fashion, so to say, as she had entered it.

Packing the luggage presented no obstacle. She had truthfully told Mrs. Saltfield that not all her effects had been removed, and it needed little effort to fill the slim carpetbag or the feather-light bonnet box. The cowhide trunk offered no difficulties beyond her scope.

Carrying the boxes was a different kettle of gray gurnard entirely.

She was able to take the two lighter ones into the hall, with its infestation of sporting prints displayed over blood-red wallpaper. Raising the cowhide piece by part of its wooden frame was nearly impossible, and moving the infernal contrivance was quite beyond the strength of any one person this side of Hercules. She had mulishly determined not to ask for help, but circumstances had overpowered her.

It didn't occur to Miranda that the use of the bellpull near the bed would bring some servant running to wait upon her and others as needed. As a result she went back to the hall to shout for help.

The placing of two luggage pieces had attracted the attention of Pam, the bulldog. At sight of Miranda, however, the animal refrained from sniffing around the new manifestation and turned to her. Courtesy and affection caused her to accept Pam's unspoken declaration of eternal fealty and love. By the time she was able to prod the noisy beast in another direction it had crossed her mind that everyone on the domestic staff had possibly gone to sleep for the balance of this morning.

She called, "Mr. Grimm, Mr. Grimm!"

There was a pause, and then footsteps could be heard as vigorously as if they were proceeding up the close and down the stair of the celebrated doggerel which had always frightened her in childhood. Instead of being confronted by Burke or Hare on the way to that session of the Scottish assizes in which they would be sent to their well-deserved doom, it was only the overweight butler who appeared in front of her.

"What would be wanted, miss?" Grimm was wheezing as a result of having answered what might be an urgent summons.

"I need help." Miranda pointed inside to the heavy luggage. "I am leaving."

The butler's face showed no approval or regret. It was not his task to express feelings about the caprices of those whose needs he was hired to fill.

"This big one has to be taken to the street while I find a growler to ride me to the St. Pancras station."

"Ah, miss, much as I would like to be of service myself, more than one man is required for such a task."

"Can somebody else on the staff be enlisted?" She knew that the domestic staff bristled with a steward, four footmen, a coachman, a groom, and a stable helper. There was even a head gardener, implying that at least one under gardener was also employed, but she didn't understand the need for those latter functionaries at all.

"The staff will be available, to be sure." Grimm paused, squinting. "Not immediately, however, miss. Most of the staff has been sent out as usual to perform various morning errands, which I fear is my doing and Mrs. Jossy's as well." He was referring to the dour housekeeper, whom Miranda had seen from a distance.

"In that case, I will find a coach and the driver can come up and get that luggage down with your help."

It was the work of a moment for Miranda to turn, having already gripped the lower part of her unfashionable dress to raise it. She ran past gewgaws and paintings on the walls. Descending the long narrow curved staircase caused her no difficulty whatever. At her age and under the present circumstances, she was almost able to run as she moved.

A commotion could be heard as she reached the lowest step. Her eyes were turned in anticipation toward the nearest door, so she cannoned into the Earl of Wingham. Her breath, which had been coming satisfactorily until she identified the source of the impact, was beginning to emerge only with astonishing difficulty.

Wingham, like Miranda, was halted. The collision had disarranged tufts of his dark hair. Those deep blue eyes of his were narrowed in a squint. Remembering yesterday's crush on Savile Street, he found himself thinking that his acquaintance with this young girl had been punctuated by traffic disturbances.

"You're not to leave," he said when it became possible for him to get the words out.

Miranda found his *diktat* forbidding indeed. Possible guesses about what was in his mind caused her to pull back.

"I—I shall scream for help."

"I see no need for that." Lionel was insistent because he had already experienced the sound of feminine voices in various unearthly registers over the last moments.

Miranda couldn't have known about the Earl's temporarily fragile eardrums, but she was well aware that he hadn't made a move in her direction. The dread of encountering a fate worse than death, whatever that might consist of, receded.

Charlotte Dempster suddenly said, accusation in the tones, "You frightened her!"

"Not in the least." Lionel was emphatic. "Are you frightened of me, Miranda?"

"No."

"Not at all?"

"Absolutely not."

"It took her a moment to answer that last question," Charlotte pointed out, concerned that Miranda was being oppressed at the hands of a male. "You know it did!"

"This is not the area in which to discuss sensitive matters," Lionel snapped, shifting the rhetorical ground to an issue that couldn't possibly be argued differently.

It was an order, in effect. Charlotte Dempster emerged from the door to the large sitting room, prepared to lower her voice at least. In a rose dress with smutched sleeves, she looked lovely. Behind her, features suspiciously straight, was Mrs. Faustine Saltfield.

"We will adjourn to—ah, the small sitting room."

Miranda allowed herself to look puzzled.

"All of us," Lionel added firmly.

The look of puzzlement remained on Miranda's features as if it had been engraved.

"I have made a fresh decision about your future," said the Sovereign's Right Trusty and Right Well-Beloved Cousin. "Simple justice alone demands that you should know what it is."

Lionel eased himself into the gent's chair, which allowed him an excellent view of half a dozen houseplants on an octagonal table, ostrich feathers in vases, varicolored fans on the walls, and a black-and-gold music stool with uncompleted sewing instead of music sheets inside. Charlotte took the stuffed sofa, where Mrs. Saltfield joined her after a silent invitation.

Miranda was unable to sit and elected to stand before the black-and-white Japanese screen which secluded a tile grate for no known reason. It crossed her mind, not for the first time, that Lionel's decisive practicality made him a far more handsome man, a thought which no one else in the room could have fathomed.

"You are to be married," Lionel began abruptly, unaware of any need to equivocate.

On the verge of a riposte along the lines that every woman was certainly intending to marry, Miranda halted. Her breath caught yet again. Never would she have expected such a proposal, eliminating the most obvious and delectable areas of courtship. Further, if marriage between himself and Miranda was already on the Earl's level head, surely Miss Dempster, his affianced, would not have been permitted to give her implicit approval to the proceedings.

It was Faustine Saltfield who first interpreted the reasons for Miranda's perplexity. "A young man is to be found who will suffice for the purpose."

"You don't mean someone at home?"

"Not in Kent." Lionel was shaking his head, mildly irritated. "Here in the City."

Miranda's imagination, making itself felt adversely, caused her to ask fearfully, "Do you mean that no matter how vile a man may be, no matter how base and abominable, I must marry him?"

"I am not seriously suggesting that you go off with some navvy out of Southwark." Lionel sounded temperate, but the effort showed in his briefly drawn lips. "The young man, whoever he may be, will have been thoroughly vetted as if he were under consideration for the Elgin Commission itself."

Miranda could conceive only one objection to the schedule that was being worked out to occupy the balance of her life but considered it far more politic to say nothing about that.

"Until my nuptials," she hazarded cautiously, "will I be permitted to stay in this—this lovely house?"

Lionel was touched by the agitation she was trying so unsuccessfully to conceal. Heaven alone knew what horrors the poor child could be constructing inwardly.

Charlotte, however, spoke first. "Yes, Miranda, for the very brief period that must of course be involved."

Miranda understood full well that it was Miss Dempster who had prodded Lionel into making the original decision about sending her away. No doubt the reasons had been sound, from Miss Dempster's particular point of view. Miranda felt sympathetic. Indeed it was impossible even now to bear the slightest animosity toward the attractive blond Londoner whose concern was reflected so clearly in her admirable features.

Lionel stood up. It was his laudable goal to pat Miranda comfortingly, at first on an arm. Charlotte Dempster was apparently disturbed by the proximity putting him face-to-face with Miranda. He stepped to one side so that he wasn't making eye contact but still felt himself moved, more than the others, by Miranda's uncertainty. Encouragingly he touched her on a shoulder. Miss Dempster, observing the gesture, stiffened noticeably.

At this point Miranda acted before he could pull away once again, mostly because of very real affection, to say the least of it, and partly out of gratitude, as well as expressing the pleasure she felt in the knowledge that she would remain in his company, certainly for a while longer.

She moved to face Lionel, then thrust both arms around him and raised herself to administer a sisterly kiss on a cheek and nothing more in light of the witnesses to her actions. Lionel abruptly moved his head as though to let his affianced know without words that he was manfully attempting to break away. As a result, however, his lips were located where the cheek had been and Miranda's lips promptly met his.

From what seemed like a distance she heard a sudden hiss that resembled steam ejected from the chimney, or whatever it was called, of a moving train. Charlotte Dempster had accompanied that unintentional mimicry by surging to her feet.

It was Mrs. Saltfield, moving like a dancer going to reverse in the course of a valse, who drew Miranda aside. The task was accomplished with great precision.

Miranda recovered herself before anyone else in the room, saying breathily to a dazed Lionel, "I wanted to thank you, thank you for everything you'll be doing for me while we're under the same roof."

She didn't hear Charlotte's gasp, nor would she have known why Miss Dempster found herself reacting in such a fashion.

Mrs. Saltfield, placing a hand at Miranda's shoulder and an even stronger hand at her back, was firmly and persistently steering her to the door.

"It is time that we were leaving now, dear, to do the day's shopping just as was originally planned," Mrs. Saltfield remarked while in motion.

Having been banished from the small sitting room, Miranda,

of course, didn't see the Right Honorable, the Earl of Wingham, attempting to recover his equilibrium. Nor was she a witness to that legendary tight smile with which Charlotte Dempster invariably showed tension.

"There is a problem with that young lady and it had better be solved as soon as may be," Charlotte said. "For all our sakes, I believe."

But as Charlotte looked at the disconcerted Lionel, dear Lionel, she was thinking that perhaps she herself was the one with a problem.

Miranda was well aware of an occasional amused look from Mrs. Saltfield during tne carriage ride on the start of this shopping safari. If the older woman thought that Miranda had behaved with admirable spirit, she kept it to herself. Miranda looked out the window of the medical brougham in which his lordship had been riding when he first met her. The coachman negotiated pitfalls in the Strand with a facility he had completely failed to show on the previous occasion.

"Is this the location in which we'll be shopping for clothes?" she asked incredulously as the carriage halted in the Lowther Arcade, where it seemed as if nothing was sold but toys.

"Indeed yes," said Mrs. Saltfield, making herself heard above the voices of eager children, petulant governesses, and short-tempered mothers. "Mademoiselle Beryl, a modiste of British birth, I grant, but quite as efficient as any Frenchy, has her emporium hereabouts."

The lady's business premises were located between a shop called The Toyman and another that was more elliptically designated as Noah's Ark. The lady herself was a toothy creature who had at one time been forty years of age and whose youth it was impossible even for Miranda to imagine. She welcomed Mrs. Saltfield with purrs but clucked over Miranda's costume as insultingly as Miranda had ever anticipated.

"Put yourself in my hands, little girl, and you'll soon be able to swell it in the City," she said in an accent as French as might be heard from a native of Tunbridge Wells.

In her sullen anger, Miranda approved only one of the day dresses that were shown to her.

"The others are obviously suitable, too," her cicerone insisted, "and I will purchase all three of them."

"And I, in turn, will wear only one of them, ever."

The modiste, who was nobody's fool, became aware of the cause of her problem. Deftly she exerted herself to see that Miranda was offered the most appropriate merchandise that graced her inventory.

No patron could have denied that the parade of evening dresses and cloaks Miranda was now shown was certain to enhance the red-haired attractiveness that London men saw in her. One or two of them would even minimize the chin that she conceived of as jutting monstrously.

Miranda relented and gave her agreement to other purchases that were contemplated for her by Mrs. Saltfield. Stubbornness reappeared in her once again, however, when she tried a pair of dark-heeled button-up shoes.

"They don't fit," she reported, having taken several steps on a tartan carpet to confirm her impression.

"I can show you other items from our special stock," the modiste offered.

Miranda was able to conclude in a little while that Mademoiselle Beryl's special stock of footwear may have been designed for human creatures, but not for Miranda Powell, late of Ryehurst in Kent.

"My objection remains," she said after the sixth pair had been discarded. "None of them fit."

"I'm sure that changes could be made," Mrs. Saltfield suggested, wanting to make another purchase in this establishment where she was treated almost like the dear Queen.

"Of course, but not to any good effect," Miranda insisted. "These shoes give no indication that they would ever fit me."

The two older women exchanged glances. Mademoiselle Beryl, having achieved victory with most of the garments that had been offered, accepted defeat with a shrug.

"I shall take you to the Angel and Three Shoes in Crambourn Alley," Mrs. Saltfield said. "If John Snowdon cannot satisfy you with shoes or boots or pumps, then resign yourself to trudging barefoot up and down London."

An image of herself dressed impeccably but without footwear appropriate to the City flashed in Miranda's mind. Her qualms faded for once after less than a minute. The mental picture was too ridiculous.

"It can't be allowed to come to that," she murmured, amused.

Mrs. Saltfield chuckled in response. "Stubborn as can be, aren't you?" she smiled, although it would have been a matter of dispute as to which of them had attempted to be more intractable. "You couldn't be anyone but your father's daughter, I know it! Joseph was exactly the same, exactly!"

Miranda smiled back. A compliment had been intended, but she wondered if the inability to compromise could generally be considered a desirable trait. She supposed that it couldn't but answered the objection by saying that on this occasion she had been entirely in the right.

The recent discussion had certainly been of a minor nature, but its course helped confirm Miranda's growing faith in her own judgment. In a far more important matter, one which concerned her future, she also remained convinced, and almost certainly with justice, that she was entirely in the right.

CHAPTER SEVEN

Charlotte Draws a Beau at a Venture

Half an hour's worth of discussions between Charlotte and her affianced brought them no nearer toward achieving a solution to their great difficulty. Whenever Charlotte suggested a likely husband for Miranda Powell, dear Lionel, as she always thought of him, offered some objection. Charlotte retired from the discussion at last. Unlike her affianced, however, she had arrived at a partial decision, if not a choice.

For it seemed to her that a swain had to appear as a fait accompli. Let Miranda be offered for, and swiftly, and Lionel could under no circumstances decline, not if he wanted to retain his diplomatic position and rise even higher in that particular sphere.

One objection did occur to Charlotte. It was possible that none of the swains who had been mentioned in the course of the recent pourparlers would be considered acceptable, if only because dear Lionel might feel he had already rejected them for Miranda's sake. Which meant that some other male had to be hauled into this matter by the scruff of his reputation, a male of good family and prepared to offer for Miranda almost as soon as he met her. It followed, then, that the candidate had to be as bereft of the needful, of finances, as Charlotte's parents.

It was a tall order.

Charlotte wanted time to consider these developments and proceeded by cab to one place where a meed of privacy could be hers. The cab halted at last in front of the Hotel Ibbetson, a breath from Oxford Street. As ever, the premises were infested by visiting university types to whom it was a substitute quad.

Clergymen often stayed at the Ibbetson as well. In both cases, the relatively inexpensive rates were the greatest lure. Charlotte's parents had been drawn to the Ibbetson by the same consideration. Unlike those others, however, Mr. and Mrs. Dempster, accompanied by their offspring, remained in residence all year round.

Her parents were taking their ease in the sitting room of the suite. Mrs. Dempster, a small woman whose once-blond hair had grayed, was engaged with a needle and thread. Mr. Dempster, bald and with gray eyes like his daughter's, was reading the *Economist.* His teeth were gritted, a gesture Charlotte identified effortlessly as she had often seen it in him. It meant that he was bitter at the notion of investment opportunities denied him only because previous forays into the marketplace had depleted the family's reserves almost to the vanishing point.

"If only you were a gambler," Mrs. Dempster was saying, not, alas, for the first time. Her voice had never been musical, as Charlotte's was considered, and it was a cause of fervent speculation *en famille* about the source of their daughter's speaking gift. "You can explain to a gambler that he is on his way to perdition and all society agrees. But in your case, you only want to do what others have done and made their fortunes at. What can one say except that you are unlucky and don't know it? The same objection as holds true for a gambler. You remain a sore trial to your nearest and dearest."

Not for the first time, either, Mr. Granville Dempster said, "Here is an added investment opportunity that is golden, Edna, simply golden!"

"Indeed."

"This man, Wood by name, has invented what is called a hypodermic syringe to inject liquid medicine under the skin. There are millions of pounds to be made in buying shares of this product, my dear, I am certain."

"It doesn't matter. We hardly have money enough to invest in this hotel suite for the purpose of renting it much longer."

"If I didn't know that, my dear, you would certainly have brought it to my attention even more often than you have done.

What I was saying is that the possibility of earning a fortune is enough to make my head spin."

"Foh! Anyone who needs to take a medicine can swallow it."

"But my dear Edna, what if a person has swooned or is otherwise not able to swallow?"

"That person cannot have any need of a medication until he or she revives," Mrs. Dempster pointed out, severely. "Until then, whoever it may be can most assuredly wait."

"My dear, that isn't—"

"This hypnotic syringe, or whatever it may be, will be no more useful than some of the other alleged inventions into which you have dumped our money. Who else would buy stock shares in a firm that claims to have invented a printing telegraph? And what about the firm with what you call a steel converter?"

"I still have faith in those two investments, my dear, and many others."

"Faith indeed! The most niggling sharper with a smooth lying tongue can convince you to put money into ridiculous so-called inventions which will never see the light of day."

Charlotte, having by now divested herself of an azure cloak, stood with feet apart at a point halfway between the contenders.

"I wonder if I may discuss a practical matter in which help is needed immediately," she said.

The Dempsters, well aware that their future was dependent on Charlotte as far as could be seen, desisted from further quarreling at this time. Charlotte, with their attention now assured, explained the dilemma which had been brought about by dear Lionel's hesitations and worries concerning Miss Miranda Powell.

"I mean to bring in someone who has not yet been considered as husband material and will be above reproach as well," she concluded.

"Who?" Mrs. Dempster asked.

Charlotte allowed herself a sigh. "That is exactly the question I was intending to put before my esteemed progenitors."

Mr. Dempster, recognizing the extent of the problem, was

first with a suggestion. "What about the Passys' grandson? The youngest, I mean. That one who is maritally uncommitted." The Baron had loaned considerable money to his old friend and would surely come to their aid with the use of a grandson, Mr. Dempster assumed.

"Herbert, you mean? He is either thirteen or fourteen years old. Big for his age, I grant, but he simply won't do for an obvious reason."

Mrs. Dempster said, "Has any thought been given to what's-his-name Coverdale?"

"Rupert? He is of an age, certainly, but he drinks far too much."

"What about Joshua Speedicutt's boy?" Mr. Dempster made that suggestion and gave a sudden snap of two fingers at the same time.

"He will always be too much of a ladies' man," Charlotte said, a little coolly. "I will not have Miss Powell married to someone who can only cause painful complications in her life."

Mrs. Dempster, bemused, put in, "So you are planning a happy marriage for this girl."

Mr. Dempster's bald head rose immediately. He wished he could be alone with Edna to get a new argument under way.

"I see nothing wrong with a happy marriage," Charlotte responded vigorously. "I plan upon having one with dear Lionel."

"Wingham is a most exceptional man," Mrs. Dempster said promptly and sincerely, distracted in spite of herself from the beckoning fray. "Do you know anyone else at all like him? In that, Charlotte, may lie the solution to this quandary."

"Of course I don't," Charlotte snapped, loyal to her affianced as ever. "I am acquainted with a pleasant-spoken man or two, a good-natured man or two, but not . . ."

Mr. Dempster asked, "What is it?"

"Just possibly, Mother may have given me an idea," Charlotte said and turned to the nearest wardrobe. From this she once again brought out her azure cloak. "I can only hope that he is in the City, as time is extremely valuable."

And she rushed away, absorbed by the need for urgency. It occurred to her later that she ought to return and tell her

Love Is a Scandal

parents exactly who she planned to see and why, but she was unsettled at the prospect of taking that many added minutes. Certainly she would make up for such unfilial behavior with a full report when she came back.

Mr. and Mrs. Dempster, alone at last, resumed quarreling. It was one of the bonds between them, and a familiar feeling made it almost comfortable to sit and joust in their own fashion.

Progress was likely to be made more efficiently after a brisk walk, it seemed to Charlotte. Many purposeful strides took her to Stephen's Hotel in Bond Street. This was a reasonably priced caravanserai always chockablock with Army officers in their spangled blue-and-white uniforms. At the desk she asked to meet *Mr.* (she lingered over that title) Oswald Badger in the downstairs room.

The aforementioned Oswald Badger took only a few minutes to join Charlotte in the meeting room, which was known to the Army patrons as the parade ground. He was an unmarried male of reasonably good character. His immediate family had died out a while ago, and the distant connections were not interested in assisting a young man who would live nowhere but in London. As one result, Oswald was perpetually on his uppers. Seeing the pleasure that lighted his eyes at her appearance, Charlotte wondered if it wasn't a mutual need for money that had kept the two of them from marriage. In the situation that prevailed, she wouldn't hesitate for a moment to graft Oswald, so to say, onto Miss Powell.

"Ah, it's you!" he said cheerily. He was the sort of easygoing young man with whom one couldn't imagine sustaining a series of interlocking quarrels, as her parents had been doing for many years. "And what brings you to this den of iniquity?" asked the only civilian who was registered at Stephen's.

"The opportunity to do a good deed." She couldn't resist a moment's bantering with him despite the urgency of her mission.

"You interest me strangely," Oswald grinned, swooping down on the nearest chair. His gray lounge coat stirred, moving the white shirt and blue bow tie as he crossed his legs as if adding another X to the ones already defacing his checkered trousers. "Speak."

"I will put the matter baldly or, if questioned, in a more hairy fashion." She never spoke that frivolously except to Oswald and wondered uneasily if he knew it. "You need a rich wife and I need a rich husband. My problem, as you certainly know, is almost solved."

"If your father had retained such moneys as were entailed to him," Oswald said a little dreamily for once, "who knows what solutions might have been available to both of us?"

Charlotte almost wished she hadn't divested herself of the azure cloak, in which case she could have hugged it a little more tightly around herself and concealed her fine figure.

"I have the perfect—or second most perfect, if you prefer—solution."

"You have discovered someone?"

"Yes."

"And is this female prepared to venture forth with me to matrimony and its sacrificial altar?"

"She will be."

"In which case, she must be an outlander and not at all used to London ways or mine, which are roughly similar. I have scoured the social deeps of my native city. Is it possible that this female is an aborigine?"

"She hails from Kent."

"Another suspicion is confirmed."

"She will almost certainly want to stay in London now that she has sampled its pleasures."

"And I can only hope that she does not have a close relative who will feel that I am useless." He added bitterly, "One would think that a man had to be a shelf bracket and therefore functional in order to become a good husband."

"This time no protest can be made," Charlotte said, a little more grimly than intended.

"Is she—ah, *enceinte?*"

"Certainly not."

Oswald considered. "My various offers to embark upon matrimony with girls of wealth have been rejected by parents, uncles, or aunts and once by a butler and a tweeny making certain significant gestures to their employer. The girls themselves don't reject me as a potential mate."

"I do not wish to hear about your mesmeric successes with members of my sex," Charlotte said emphatically. "To continue, then, it is my affianced's ward who needs to be married off."

Oswald surprised her by looking crestfallen. "Guardians are not as forthcoming as parents, who, I understand from various happily married friends, will run if necessary to the aid of a son-in-law in financial distress."

"You might find it a little more difficult to raise what you need, but I will be at Lionel's side and pleading effectively on your behalf." For once she wasn't calling her affianced "dear Lionel" in the presence of another. "He is not ungenerous, as you may have heard."

"Let me think," he said, then broke the silence almost immediately. "It cannot be considered a major drawback, but I feel sure that the girl can't be as attractive as someone else I might name but won't."

"Miranda is a comely girl," Charlotte said truthfully, turning from his fixed stare at her. "I wouldn't try to foist you off upon some female who would repel you."

"No, I suppose not." He looked away with difficulty but clearly remained dubious about the transaction.

"Before you render a decision, I think I ought to explain—"

"I was dreading it. There *is* something. The girl is perfectly presentable except that she has one eye in the center of her forehead."

"No, no, you fool! Please let me go on. Miranda must be wed quickly." She clarified that point in the confident knowledge that Oswald, of all people, wouldn't make a truly ill-timed jest and certainly not one about so agonizing a difficulty. "An offer for her hand in marriage must materialize almost immediately."

"Do you mean that upon being introduced I have to smile and bow and say 'I-am-honored-to-meet-you-I-wish-to-offer-for-you'?"

"It will be better if you take a powerful grip on Miss Powell and force her to accompany you to Gretna Green for an instantaneous ceremony of marriage," Charlotte said. "In the circumstances, however, a few pleasantries will do upon being introduced and for only very shortly thereafter."

Oswald looked around indecisively. A pair of deeply tanned Army men were leaving the room. One of them, his voice raised, was talking about thugs in India. The other, almost at the same time, had started to tell what was bound to be a dull anecdote about some incident involving a havildar out at Poona.

"Fine fellows, but not as steady company in my lodgings," Oswald said eventually and shrugged. "I suppose it is necessary for me to be taken to the mound of stones and tied up and then be set afire."

Charlotte understood him well enough to know that he was agreeing, in his fashion, to offer for Miranda Powell a short while after meeting her.

"There is no choice, no real choice," he added moodily. "She may be someone I would like, this girl Miranda, but you can believe me that if there did happen to be a choice—"

He bounded out of the chair, raised Charlotte swiftly, and fastened his lips to hers. Taken by surprise, she was unable to move her head away in time and then found herself responding almost against her will. There was a sound of gasping from the direction of the door, and she was abruptly freed of his embrace.

She looked at him with the beginnings of dizziness almost as acute as Lionel had felt back when Miranda kissed him. The feeling turned to near anger, but Charlotte couldn't identify the cause as being her own powerful regret that he had never settled himself. He had once reminded her, Charlotte vaguely recalled, that his late father, a banker, had worked from dusk to dawn nearly seven days a week and lost his money all the same. At the time she had considered the knowledge as another bond between them, along with having been born to impoverished male parents. She had not previously linked his family history to an understanding of his wastrel ways.

Oswald, for his part, discerned the anger in Charlotte's eyes. The reason for it, however, eluded him altogether.

"As you realize, I am your most humble obedient," he said, hiding his own distress with amiability. Then he whispered, "In all things, ever."

Charlotte turned and hurried off at long last.

CHAPTER EIGHT

A Pearl Before Swains

Miranda had never looked more lovely than in the russet ball dress with the low bodice, the slim waistline, and that expanded lower half. Dainty-heeled shoes, finally purchased in the shop called the Angel and Three Shoes, added to the effect. With Charlotte Dempster's encouragement, she had added a trace of kohl powdering to her slim brows, darkening them and accordingly giving an effect of even greater brightness emanating from her center-parted fiery red hair.

In full fig, therefore, she was being taken to her first London ball.

A silent Lionel and the two ladies accompanied her, watching as she climbed out of the brougham at eleven o'clock on this night. It was a splendid time to make an appearance. While other revelers had been at different parties or the opera or theatre, Miranda and the coven of female advisers had been helping to put additional touches to the effect given by herself in this finery. Lionel, pacing below in the large sitting room at Jermyn Street, had considered his diplomatic efforts with the Elgin Commission and nothing else.

All had traveled to Lower Brook Street. The region was cluttered with houses, a residential block more crowded at night than the business street of Ryehurst at high noon. Miranda had been told the names of their host and hostess, but in her excitement she hadn't retained the information.

"And now what?" she asked tautly as they stood in front of the door.

"From now on," said Lionel, amused out of his preoccupation

by the excitement in her voice, "you wait until the prince appears in order to fit the missing slipper to one of your feet."

Miranda couldn't be seen blushing. Some such recollection had certainly occurred to her, except that she was hoping for a male far closer to her current home than Prince Charming of the legend.

With only a glance to the clutter of the hallway once the four of them had been admitted, she followed the other women to a room at the foot of white-painted stairs. Here, in the presence of a perky young maid, they left their cloaks.

Miranda couldn't help looking around anxiously. "But where are the dressing rooms?"

Charlotte, more attractive even than usual in her pale yellow with black dashes placed strategically, gave a discreet smile at what she felt was *gaucherie* on Miranda's part. Mrs. Saltfield, expecting Joseph Powell's daughter not to be at a loss in whatever company she might find herself, waxed mildly sarcastic.

"You are not in the country now, with special rooms in which to change shoes, to brush the hair, or pin ribbons on or add fresh flowers to one's costume," she said a little tartly. "Here in London we proceed to the ballroom immediately upon arriving."

Miranda did find a moment to press the flat of a palm down against the top of her head but felt certain it wasn't of the slightest benefit to her appearance.

Another surprise awaited her immediately. Having expected to enter the ballroom on Lionel's arm, or perhaps with herself on one arm and Charlotte on the other, she was positioned instead before Mrs. Saltfield and with Charlotte and Lionel in single file in back of them. It reminded her of some odious parade of devout animals as illustrated on the wallpaper in the bedroom she had been allotted at the Jermyn Street house.

She gave her name to the incurious footman at the head of the stairs. He shouted up, "Miss Miranda Parl." Slowly she walked to the first landing, where another footman, turned to the direction of the ballroom, shouted, "Miss Janet Pell." A butler who looked as if he had not long ago been mummified nodded at the bulletin and announced, "Miss Janet Poll." Miranda supposed it would have to do.

The lady who employed three at least partially deaf servants was standing just inside the doorway. She smiled vivaciously, a middle-aged woman with merry eyes. "I am so pleased to meet you, and I feel sure I will eventually have the straight of your name."

It was a hope that Miranda reciprocated. She had the suspicion that a title was part of it and felt convinced that there was a husband in the family. Of this latter, however, there was no sign. Not till afterwards was she to be apprised of the town custom by which only the wife and daughters greeted guests while the husband and sons enjoyed themselves among those visitors whose company they preferred.

"I am most pleased to be here," Miranda said truthfully, her smile far from the usual polite mask.

A dance card was given her upon leaving the hostess, but no implement with which to inscribe the names of those who applied for the privilege of a whirl about the floor in her company. It seemed typical of what ought to have been a glorious night, but one in which varied factors had combined to keep her slightly off balance.

Mrs. Saltfield shortly materialized at her side, attractive in a quiet and properly discreet royal blue. Charlotte took exactly the correct amount of time with their hostess, and Lionel followed. Miranda observed that the hostess, after speaking with Lionel, stole a look out at the attendees, most likely for another inspection of the young lady she now knew as the Earl's ward.

A young man turned at the sight of her, smiled, and approached.

"May I be given the privilege of a dance with you?"

Miranda didn't have any objection, but she knew an opportunity when it came up. Seeing Lionel "arming" Charlotte on the way to the dance floor she said clearly, "You have to obtain permission from my guardian."

Lionel, as a result, was unable to attempt dancing with Charlotte. He agreed to let the young man have his fling. Miranda made a mental note of his name and assigned him a late number.

An older man came over, grinning. "I cannot permit such a

dainty morsel to pass through the gates of my home without requesting a dance."

"Of course," Miranda smiled.

Lionel had to agree, and she let herself be escorted out to the floor by the hostess's husband.

"Please excuse my abysmal ignorance," she said as the band girded its collective loins for a polka, "but I don't know your name."

"I am Marmont. Because of my late father's ability to make a friend of the late George the Fourth, I am also a duke." He chuckled. "And you, I understand from another, are Wingham's ward."

"Yes."

"Ah." The Duke of Marmont winked an eye. "A down cove is young Wingham. He is certain to be a comer in the Diplomatic."

The words weren't familiar, but Miranda's lively imaginative faculties permitted her to understand their meaning. The Duke was already convinced that Lionel had imported so attractive a young lady for certain sub rosa purposes which were only hinted at but never directly mentioned in what passed for good society.

The dance was eventually concluded, and Miranda was armed back to Mrs. Saltfield. Charlotte had by this time persuaded Lionel onto the square of dance floor, and they were doing the valse with great verve.

She had lost her appetite for flirting with other males in order to rouse feelings of jealousy in Lionel. To name only one objection, the Earl was out of her immediate sight. More important, however, she could now visualize one male sniggering to another that Wingham's pretty ward must be free with her favors. The temptation to turn her back on the assemblage was one that Miranda knew would have to be rejected for Lionel's sake alone.

All the same, when two young men separately asked permission for dances, she gestured Mrs. Saltfield to decline for her.

Lionel's aunt must have signaled him back from the dance floor in consequence. Charlotte, of course, accompanied him.

"Miranda has refused a pair of potential suitors," Lionel's Aunt Saltfield said.

Lionel, brows drawn, managed to respond, "Perhaps there is some reason we don't know."

He was waiting for an explanation. It crossed Miranda's mind to say that if he would dance with her the truth would be revealed. Lionel did not now seem in the proper mood for sporting a toe. Apparently he wanted the matter of an offer for Miranda to be settled with the least difficulty, perhaps not even to see whatever young man might be first to avail himself of Miranda's services as a wife.

"You can choose any partner who seems suitable," Charlotte said pacifically. "For anyone who asks, however, give a number and later say that you are indisposed, if you still have no wish for that individual's company. But I do plead with you not to refuse anyone out of hand."

Charlotte had spoken with considerable emphasis. At any moment now, according to the arrangement she had concocted early this afternoon in a wholly businesslike missive to Oswald Badger, that young man himself was going to materialize and work his wiles on Miranda.

She didn't have long to wait. Oswald arrived in moments. To a canary yellow waistcoat, gleaming white shirt, and violet tie, he had added white trousers and cherry-red evening slippers. This concoction of ill-matching wear he paraded with such panache that no one looked twice at him except with unfeigned admiration.

He paused, his eyes taking in Charlotte and the best finery in her possession. Briefly their glances met. Charlotte forced a welcoming smile and then looked away, turning to Lionel for a remark about the quality of the band music that the Marmonts' hired musicians were purveying.

Charlotte's letter had informed Badger that the girl he was seeking would wear russet, and this proved to be correct. The young girl's general aura of freshness, although it wasn't likely to win Oswald's admiration over a long period of time, was fetching upon first sight. He found himself looking forward to a smile from her full red lips.

"We've not met," he said to Miranda, having shrewdly decided to engage her in conversation rather than requesting a dance at some later time. "Are you new to London?"

He didn't see that Lionel had turned from Charlotte to examine him in a hostile manner. Miranda, having observed the phenomenon, made her tones and features agreeably vivacious.

"I hail from Kent, as it happens, but hope to stay in the City forever."

"I've visited Kent on occasion." Oswald had visited almost all of Britain once or twice. He was a superb guest, well mannered, ever courteous, helpful to a distraught hostess. "A friend of mine lives near the Romney marshes, and except for an occasional wheeze as a result he is delighted by the ambience."

"I don't know that particular area very well, I'm afraid."

"You are equally, or almost equally, a stranger to London balls, I take it. There is some difficulty in knowing when to accept a man's offer for a dance."

"Difficulty, but not impossibility." She was a little cooler now that Lionel was out of earshot.

Oswald had noticed with a stab of envy that Charlotte and her affianced were on the nearby dance floor together. During a turn in the polka, Charlotte's eyes raked Miranda and him. He didn't see Lionel's eyes in their direction when it was the Earl who faced them, but Miranda couldn't help being aware of that.

"Now I," Oswald continued, reminded of the need to ingratiate himself further with Miss Powell, "I am one to accept as soon as may be."

"For what reason, sir?"

"Because I am rather an unusual male."

"I cannot feel sure that you are offering a recommendation."

"Yes, one appreciates that point. If a male unicorn or a walrus were to approach and ask for a dance, you would hesitate."

"Not at all. I would favor him with a late number on my card, and when the claimant approached I would pretend that I was indisposed."

"Some finer points of etiquette have traveled the length and breadth of the kingdom, I am glad to hear. I need not point out, however, that I am neither a unicorn nor a walrus. I am, indeed, rather a fine dancer."

Miranda had no wish to encourage the young man by involving him in further persiflage. "I am afraid that the request has to be made to my guardian, if you decide to pursue this matter."

The dance had come to an end. Lionel, although not at all winded, was leaving the dance floor and walking toward Miranda. It made no difference that Charlotte had strongly indicated how much she would have liked to continue dancing with him.

Miranda turned immediately. "I have been asked for a dance by Mr.—this gentleman."

She had rather hoped that the newcomer, aware of her chilly tones, had taken himself off. In this, however, she was disappointed.

"Oswald Badger. Your most humble obedient, miss, sir."

Lionel grunted, reminding himself that the object of the exercise, when all was said and done, remained that of finding a presentable mate for his ward.

"In that case," said Oswald, hardly daunted by a lack of civility, "I beg leave to claim my dance now."

No alternative presented itself to anyone. Miranda, accordingly, was armed out to the floor. During the brisk canter, as she wryly thought of the dignified march to the dance area that seemed to her no larger than a pair of one-penny blacks end to end, she gave her name upon request. Oswald had already known it but was just as pleased that the matter should be confirmed by an unimpeachable source.

"Do you go the wrong way?" he asked while they waited for the musicians to unleash yet another selection.

"I beg your pardon?" Miranda was unnerved.

"While dancing the valse," Oswald pursued, clarifying the matter and eliminating the source of Miranda's uncertainty, "do you perform the reverse?"

"Why, of course."

"I was afraid of that," he said dolefully. "In Kent and the Romney Marshes, as I recollect, going the wrong way in valse is all the crack, as my late guv'nor used to say. Here in the City, however, it is considered shocking."

Miranda was startled by the explanation. "But in the polka everybody reverses. I just saw them doing it on this very floor."

"For the polka, that maneuver is not thought of as *bizarre,*" Oswald said. "In the valse, for reasons that defy elucidation by a mere mortal, it is. I tell you this as you might otherwise consider me a bumble-footed clod, but I am only aping my peers by not reversing."

"Thank you for that further clarification." It was impossible not to be amused when she wasn't looking to meet Lionel's eyes yet again.

The Earl did stare in her direction, at which time she moved slightly closer to her partner. Oswald, a gentleman to the fingertips and well aware of a possible adverse reaction from bystanders, promptly moved away.

Charlotte distracted Lionel by talk. When she wasn't claiming his attention, though, Charlotte, too, was turning her head toward the dancers. A play of mixed emotions could be distinguished on her normally attractive features. Miranda wasn't surprised at herself for concluding that Charlotte's feelings about Lionel were not nearly as strong as her own.

Belatedly the musicians offered a lively galop, playing with instruments that sounded in their hands like the contents of a craftsman's case with its saws and adzes and augers. Miranda had to dance and keep her teeth gritted at the same time.

"Another dance?" Oswald Badger asked at the conclusion. "Perhaps further selections will be rendered with more timbre and less brio, so to speak."

"You must make a request of my guardian."

"But that good gentleman has agreed to one fling, and you appear to find my company not unpleasant. Furthermore, you dance deucedly well, I may add!"

"Nevertheless," she began, and felt herself whirled against her will into a polka. Aware of the penalties of making any scene, as he must have anticipated, she permitted the charade to continue.

"I believe it will be possible for me to return under my own power," she said when the dance was over.

Oswald accepted the implied rebuke for his impetuousness but walked at Miranda's side and a short distance from her.

As Lionel turned to see them drawing closer, Miranda suddenly extended an arm for him to take. Oswald obliged, of course, his mobile features showing no surprise at her sudden change of mood. He had dealt in the past with the female of the species.

"I hope to see you again before the evening is out," he said with gallantry. She did dance well.

He knew, but she didn't, that granting more than two dances on the same evening was considered in London society as tantamount to a declaration of great interest between a girl and one particular partner.

"My dance card is filled," Miranda lied calmly. It was regrettable to have had to employ the young man for her own purpose, and she could at least set him free of the thralldom to her that he apparently labored under. "Thank you, however, for asking."

"Certainly we can meet on another day, and very soon."

It seemed to Miranda that Oswald Badger couldn't bring himself to admit that his sudden powerful feelings for her weren't reciprocated. He had offered, however, what Miranda felt was an unexpected opportunity.

With no intention of pursuing the matter after this night, she waited till Lionel was in earshot and then said pleasantly, "I am certain that my guardian will agree to another meeting with the proviso that I am chaperoned."

Oswald looked sullen.

Turning to her baleful-eyed guardian, she asked, "May I be permitted to see Os— Mr. Badger, again?"

Lionel was unable to force words past his lips. He had been informed by Charlotte that the young man was a desirable candidate for Miranda's hand in marriage. Nevertheless, he couldn't bring himself to give the words of approval that would virtually cast Miranda adrift in the sea of life with some stranger. He didn't realize, of course, that he and Miranda had been strangers until a short while ago. Or perhaps he did let the thought cross his mind and then deflected it.

"Would tomorrow be suitable?" Oswald pressed eagerly. "Will you consent to a stroll about Covent Garden at noon?"

Miranda heard a sudden explosive sound issue from between Lionel's clamped lips. At Charlotte's look it ceased.

"Splendid," Miranda beamed, certain that her guardian's unwilling agreement had been given.

Charlotte, wanting to make the situation clear as a crystal, put in, "I am sure there can be no objection, Mr. Badger."

Lionel looked meaningfully at his Aunt Saltfield, who nodded.

"No objection," he said in dispirited tones. "None whatever."

Miranda had lied to the importunate Oswald, to be sure, about her dance card being filled. In a very short time, however, the card was crowded with names. Young males approached one after another and asked for the favor of a dance. Miranda, having secured a pencil, positioned most of these for a time later in the evening.

It was borne in upon her that young ladies as attractive as herself and certainly as well dressed were sitting pensively in the hallway and on the stairs. No one had asked them to sport a toe on the floor. Miranda did not conceive of herself as lovely, nor did she realize that there was freshness in her complexion and great warmth in the wide forest-green eyes. Her only feeling was a wonderment at young men being greatly attracted to a female who, it must be writ large on her face, was deeply interested in another. Miranda, as has been stated, was only seventeen years of age.

She found that feelings of resentment toward those who were neglecting her sisters, by which designation she wholeheartedly thought of the females unknown to her, wouldn't fade.

As a result, when she danced with a young man who warmly hoped for another meeting she had a ready suggestion to offer.

"Would you be suited by a walk tomorrow at noon in Covent Garden?"

"Why, yes, of course," the young man said, flustered but wholly agreeable at having ostensibly made a conquest.

To another who expressed a similar hope, Miranda offered the same suggestion. Again it was eagerly accepted.

Only a third applicant, offered the suggestion, opined that he had to work in his father's bank on the next day and at the suggested time. As Miranda didn't have the least intention of making an appearance in the designated area, she cheerily consented to put back the rendezvous to early evening.

It can be said with more than a modicum of truth that Miss Miranda Powell's first ball in London was a memorable occasion for her.

CHAPTER NINE

A Bumper Crop
in Covent Garden

Miranda always felt certain that her dreams were vivid, even if she couldn't recollect them. On this night she must have slept with unusual stress, for when somebody opened the bedroom door to wake her in the middle of morning, she called out.

"There is no need to shriek the house down," Faustine Saltfield said briskly, moving into the room. She was dressed for the daylight, in lavender that showed her slightly overweight figure to the best possible advantage and even complimented her merry blue eyes.

Not having expected a visitation, Miranda promptly dreaded bad news. "Has something happened?"

"Not yet," Mrs. Saltfield said. "Nor will it unless you first arise from your bower."

Miranda asked herself whether one more shopping trip lay ahead, or some other pleasurable duty. It was impossible to remember at this time.

"If you will permit me," Miranda started.

Mrs. Saltfield courteously looked toward the closed velvet curtains.

Miranda raised herself. The room had been altered so that books for children were eliminated along with various and sundry gewgaws. Nothing could be done on such short notice about the wallpaper with its chatting animals depicted so earnestly, but the sight of bare shelves convinced her that the advance of age had helped her achieve a partial triumph in this one special area.

Having ventured behind a Japanese screen which modestly hid her lineaments from view, Miranda dressed in a lilac poplin with a frilled collar and sleeves that seemed on the point of stopping short beyond her wrists but mercifully refrained. It was one of the modish rig-outs which had been chosen for her at Mademoiselle Beryl's, and she hoped it didn't make her look too much like a reed bunting bird.

"You were quite the belle of the ball," Mrs. Saltfield offered encouragingly. "You reminded me of the most popular girl I knew when I was that age."

Miranda did recollect having danced with many men. Not, however, with Lionel. Charlotte had been silkily and even regretfully adamant about forbidding such a contact between the ward and her guardian.

"Now it is time to meet with Mr. Badger, as you promised," Mrs. Saltfield added, no doubt beaming. "He is a young man of good family, and socially most adept."

Miranda, in the act of buttoning her left boot, suddenly felt a pall closing around her. She had indeed promised to meet with Oswald Badger, having no intention of doing so. Later on she had made the same promise to four other men and agreed to meet them all at the same place and time. Each one must be feeling sure he was the only person of the opposite sex who would be in her company. She could easily imagine herself confronted by five surly males demanding to know why she had perpetrated this social embarrassment upon them. To explain that she had felt bitter at their ignoring the other females on the premises would be useless, she felt certain.

"I believe I—I am somewhat ill."

"Are you certain of it?"

"Oh yes, absolutely."

"Then I would advise you not to dwell upon indispositions whilst flirting with Mr. Badger," Lionel's aunt said remorselessly. "The subject does nothing to attract a male."

Was it possible that Faustine Saltfield thought, even after seeing Miranda's assured behavior on the night before, that the young girl was shy with any of the male sex? Possibly Mrs. Saltfield conjectured that Miranda was unsure of herself when dealing with one man individually. It was an error, if so, that Miranda didn't choose to correct at this time.

"I have not yet broken my fast," Miranda said, seeking another cause for delay.

"A hot potato can be obtained for you to chew upon in the cab," Lionel's Aunt Saltfield said wryly. "You must hurry now."

Miranda made a point of hesitating about which cloak to choose for outdoor wear in this warm September climate. Seeing no results from the delay, Mrs. Saltfield promptly picked the first dark cloak that presented itself to her and threw it over an arm.

"Follow me," she said, mustering an imperiousness that was otherwise foreign to her nature. "You should feel certain that you are going to meet your destiny."

Miranda was wincing as Mrs. Saltfield turned to lead the way. At the bottom of the long stairs, Miranda heard the sound of papers being rustled emphatically in the large sitting room. Grateful for the excuse, she halted.

"My guardian is home," she smiled. "I must say farewell to him."

"There is hardly enough time," the older woman began.

"But I must," Miranda insisted. "You cannot deny me the right to speak with the one to whom I owe so much."

She hurried into the large sitting room.

Here, to the right of a copy of the London *Times* at which he was scowling, Lionel could be discerned. At the interruption he stopped heaping anathemas upon the head of the Thunderer's respected editor, John Thadeus Delane, and turned. His face was set. It had been his hope that one form of anguish would make him forget another which he found inexplicable, but the two had joined, so to speak, between the same walls. The fabled death of the thousand cuts, it seemed to him, was as nothing by comparison.

He couldn't help noticing that Miranda looked typically lovely and considered that she must be joyous as a result. It didn't occur to him that such pleasure as she was showing had been caused by the sight of him.

Miranda found herself enthralled, as ever, by the sight of those deep blue eyes on her. "I—I am leaving to see Mr. Badger . . ."

No comment was offered.

". . . as I have been instructed to do," she finished lamely.

"I didn't form the impression that you found Mr. Badger's company particularly onerous."

So she had been victimized, in part at least, by her own perfectly understandable attempts to rouse jealousy in him! She had been far too successful. It seemed as if Lionel had turned away from caring for her best interests and decided on good riddance to bad rubbish!

"One doesn't wish to make a gentleman ill at ease and so I was polite to Mr. Badger."

"In which case, you must do your duty now," Lionel responded, running a firm hand through his dark hair. "Even if you find it onerous you must do your duty. There is more merit in it."

He didn't seem to be speaking to her, although Miranda couldn't look beyond her own agitation to be aware that Lionel's words were directed at Lionel himself.

It was impossible to forget the first delightful meeting between them, the occasion at which they had encountered each other. Nor would she forget the kiss they had happily exchanged, even though the singular pleasure had been shared under Charlotte Dempster's astonished eyes. With that memory alone, Miranda's lips felt warm and moist.

She said quietly, "My actions today are to be carried through because of your wishes, as I understand them."

The indirect question hung in the air. Lionel told himself grimly that he wanted to have his promising career as a diplomatist and for Miranda to be happy. He wanted Charlotte's happiness, too. Hadn't he and Charlotte been close to each other since childhood? Career difficulties to one side, he knew he wasn't the first man to become aware of the impossibility of making two women sublimely happy. Such newfound knowledge, however, offered not the slightest consolation.

"What you will be doing today, Miranda, reflects my wishes," he had to agree.

She had never expected to hear those soothing tones offer a sentiment that was quite so unpalatable.

"There may not be another time to make a different decision in this matter," she told him more sharply than she had intended.

Lionel was alert. "Are you telling me circuitously that Mr. Badger might ask this speedily if he can move his relationship to you beyond the mildest of flirtations?"

His speaking was so brisk that she was certain he had become hopeful for that outcome, for a proposal on Oswald's part. Diplomat or not, inured as he was to interpreting the thoughts of others, he was not yet aware of his feelings for her. About that much she remained convinced. When the knowledge finally smote him with all the force of a revelation in some improving legend, as was bound to happen, it would be far too late for him to act. She could visualize him repenting as the first baby was born to herself and Oswald Badger. Or the second baby or third or fourth or fifth.

"*He*, at any rate, is smitten now."

Lionel fell silent. Certainly he was aware of the emphasis in Miranda's words and the clear indication that one man was attracted and prepared to do something about it.

She turned and walked slowly out the door.

Mrs. Saltfield had been instructed by Grimm that the master was intending to use his brougham during this day's efforts in the arena of diplomacy. For that reason, it would be necessary for Miranda to be escorted in a hired cab.

Seated as comfortably as might be managed in this particular growler, Mrs. Saltfield looked compassionately over at the unhappy young girl. It occurred to her that Miss Powell, Joseph's daughter, had acquired some sort of infatuation for Lionel in the few days she had been in residence at Jermyn Street. The image of an Earl marrying his ward was a romantic one but didn't involve reality in the least. The years had made Faustine, relict of the late Hubert Saltfield, an expert in the differences between romance and reality.

"Must we move ahead this quickly?"

"I fear so, child."

Miranda looked back from the window with another freshly minted objection. "I don't want to appear too early, as it would show an unseemly willingness on my part."

Which represented a valid point, to Mrs. Saltfield's way of thinking. Joseph Powell's eyes had always lit up agreeably when she came into his sight after a delay.

"We can move briefly through Hyde Park," Mrs. Saltfield agreed. "It offers a scenic view."

Further negotiations with the driver were required, causing that good lady some brief irritation. The jehu accommodated them, however, upon the promise of a greater fee.

The cab entered from Hyde Park corner and moved along the carriage road from the south side. Miranda stared at the women on horseback, some with pages running after them. Other young females, far more daring, were unescorted. One of these was leaning over to flirt with a young male among the many on foot.

"Those women!" Mrs. Saltfield's voice, high at the best of times, was sufficiently trumpet-toned now to catch the hansom driver's attention if only briefly.

"Do you know them?" Miranda asked innocently.

"Of course not," Mrs. Saltfield answered with repugnance.

From her slight experience with different levels of acceptance in London, Miranda asked, "Aren't those women socially desirable?"

"Not at all."

"Are they what my grandfather used to call, um, dollymops?"

"The less said about those women, the better." Mrs. Saltfield's voice had once again attracted the driver's attention, and this time she took advantage of it. Their diversion had unquestionably occupied ample time. "Drive to our original destination immediately."

With the grace of a fractious beast being forced into a cage at some zoo, the carriage was turned toward Oxford Street.

Mrs. Saltfield braced herself for another appeal in favor of delay. Miranda had refrained from looking out the window, and a serious aspect possessed her usually vibrant eyes.

"I can offer yet another reason for putting off the confrontation at Covent Garden," she began. "A reason you don't yet know."

"It is easy to guess," Mrs. Saltfield said, invoking the wisdom of an occasionally observant older woman. "You are not as enamored of Mr. Badger as you are of—ah, someone else."

Miranda blinked in astonishment that a woman of Mrs. Saltfield's years might understand what was in her heart.

"Life does not always permit a female to follow the course she desires." Memories of her great disappointment caused Faustine Saltfield to lower her voice sympathetically. "One doesn't always marry the man of first choice. There is happiness of a sort to be found with another, however. Please accept my assurances about that."

Miranda wanted to say that these current times might make it easier for a woman to achieve happiness and that she for one was intending to do no less. The thought would have been at least mildly inflammatory and at this time beside the point as well. It wasn't along the lines of what she had started to say.

"I realize that I must fall back upon utter frankness," she began. "Well, then, Mr. Badger isn't the only one who—well—what I am trying with some difficulty to make clear is that—I—I asked someone else to meet me at Covent Garden."

"Another male? One who you feel that your guardian would not approve?"

"I am sure that his lordship would find the man suitable." It cost Miranda an effort to admit that much. "I met him at the ball last night."

"In that case I see no difficulty—a moment, miss. Did you by some ill chance ask this other to meet you at exactly the same time as well as the same place?"

"Yes."

"That can be awkward. Surely, however, you can explain to

Mr. Badger that your heart calls elsewhere, specifically in the direction of the other nominee."

Miranda looked down in a shamefaced way at her dark-gloved hands. "I have only a pleasant warm feeling for each man and nothing more."

She had decided moments ago that it would be less time-consuming to refrain from a discussion of her reasons for inveigling, as Mrs. Saltfield would have called it, the other men. As it was, her chaperone's intelligence was fully occupied in the effort to understand the events of the previous night.

"So you have entrapped these two men in a situation that will surely set each against the other." Mrs. Saltfield's sympathies were fading. "It is an awkward brangle and no mistake, but you did cause it and will have to resolve the matter by your own skills."

"Wouldn't it be possible to avoid the meeting?"

"Possible, yes, but not courteous. I decline to permit a member of my family, even a member by adoption, to create such an awkward position for two humans who might otherwise call each other out and perhaps even cause some injury as a result of your thoughtlessness."

"I am quite sure that such a circumstance will not occur as a result of this brangle, as you refer to it."

"And why not, pray?"

Miranda looked miserable. "There is—there is yet another."

"What? A third who you asked to meet you at the same place and time?"

"I should make it clear that Mr. Badger suggested the time and place to me, and I reciprocated with all the others."

"*All* the others? Can I infer—did you have the effrontery—to issue that invitation to more men?"

"There was a fourth," Miranda said meekly.

"And a fifth, I'll be bound. It seems probable."

"I don't remember more than five."

"Merciful heavens!"

"I am almost certain that there aren't more than five gentlemen."

"One moment, young lady, one moment. If only to straighten

the difficulty out within the precincts of my own rocking intelligence, I require a synopsis of what I have heard. As an entry in the Newgate Calendar of courtship, if there was such a contrivance, it would deserve an honored place. You have inveigled (no other word will suffice) five men into this trap of yours."

"No more than five, I am almost certain. Last night was very rushed toward the end, and I found myself with a great many partners."

"If you were seeking companions for the afternoon, why did you avoid the Foot Guards? And what of the Horse Guards? The latter look splendid in blue, with white buckskin breeches and dark jackboots, not to mention a steel cuirass over every coat."

"I regret that you are displeased, but you can see I have an excellent reason for suggesting that we discreetly avoid Covent Garden this noon."

Mrs. Saltfield knitted her brows as a symbol of deep thought. After a moment she looked up. A smile was crossing her lips.

"Your fears are unwarranted, Miranda. Although the first minute or two may prove awkward, I don't think that any discourtesy will be offered, and you're certain to find a source of pleasure in seeing the men turn out for you."

It would have been true before she met Lionel, when she had been what she now considered a callow and unsophisticated child.

"The rest of London will say that you have concocted a delicious jape," Mrs. Saltfield went on, taken by the image. "Perforce you must become the talk of society, and it can be accepted by all that you are currently the most sought-after girl in London. How you could have done anything better to advance your fortunes I simply don't know!"

Miranda thought of Lionel and how she wanted him and none other to offer for her. No word passed her lips. The older woman looked irritated, having expected some pleased response.

"Perhaps you are right." Miranda couldn't force a grin but did manage a nod to placate the disappointed Faustine Saltfield, however briefly. "I bow to your superior knowledge of the ways of the world."

Miranda suddenly felt she had gone too far and unwittingly

offended the helpful lady, but there was no need to worry about it. Mrs. Saltfield looked gratified by such deference from an attractive young woman.

Miranda mustered a smile and reached out one hand to grasp Mrs. Saltfield's in companionship. Again she had a moment's suspicion that she might have been presumptuous in making a gesture of affection. Mrs. Saltfield looked startled. The meaning of Miranda's action wasn't lost upon her for long, and a gratified Miranda felt the pressure of affection returned in full measure.

The driver approached their destination by way of Maiden Lane, causing Mrs. Saltfield to point out the barbershop once owned by the father of Mr. Turner, the painter, that very edifice in which the famous son had been born. As the day didn't happen to be an active one in the fruit and vegetable market area, the small buildings of which it consisted seemed almost as quiet as racing stables in midwinter.

Mrs. Saltfield had a few imperceptive words to say about "the actors' church," as St. Paul's was known. Despite the cognomen, which she was certain must be a denigration of any house of worship, the small building was indeed attractive. Miranda agreed after only a quick look, her mind being elsewhere.

Her insides knotted as the cab halted before the sun-touched venue of Grand Opera in London. The Covent Garden Theatre was quiet from outside, and she didn't even ask herself what she would have thought of that imposing exterior if she had encountered it under circumstances of lesser difficulty.

A young man had been standing rigidly less than a hundred feet away and in front of Francis Noble's Circulating Library shop. At sight of Miranda he went into motion, a smile on his lips, gray eyes glinting. He was bright-haired and slim. Miranda's recollections of last night's proceedings were not of the clearest, as she had pointed out, but she felt certain that it was not Mr. Oswald Badger who approached so eagerly.

"So you did arrive, Miss Powell," he said, clearly delighted. "As you may imagine, the other gentlemen felt uncertain of your fidelity to any plans made in advance, but I indicated my strong belief that you would be here and come to a choice among us."

"Your faith is heartwarming." The young man's taking the matter in such good part made it possible for Miranda to pass off the incident. "I can only hope that you (and the others, of course) were not deeply offended."

"Reactions were varied," admitted the young man whose name she still didn't know. "Ivor Dimbleby was distinctly put out by what he considered your treachery and hurried away almost as soon as he saw the others. No doubt he repaired to a nearby sweating house in hopes of working off the effects of overindulgence. Sylvan Fitton loped away to St. John's Wood, where he has a female friend he suddenly decided he didn't want to keep waiting further."

"He will be sorely missed," Miranda murmured. "And the others?"

"Unless you asked a great number of men to join us, I know of only one other. The Honorable Magnus Osmay, to whom I refer, had to return ahead of schedule to the factory in which he is part owner and had come to apologize personally for such a dereliction of social duty."

Miranda winced and made a mental note to pen a brief letter to that young man, explaining that she had intended a mild jest and had not expected unselfish behavior from anyone involved.

"Magnus and his brothers, you may know, manufacture a nostrum which is intended to help women through the times of accouchement," her informant continued. "How effective it is, I am wholly unable to tell you."

She hesitated, embarrassed to admit that she didn't recall his name.

"And myself, of course, Sir Francis Upchurch's youngest son, Aubrey," said this paragon of courtesy. "My father is the well-known railway contractor. Myself, I hope to make a lasting career as a university functionary, and I dream of eventually becoming Master of Balliol."

It was a notable ambition even in the eyes of a female who knew nothing of the university world. Miranda gave him a smile of encouragement.

"Now that we know each other somewhat better," Aubrey Upchurch added with his brightest smile, "I certainly hope that there is cause for a continued meeting of the minds."

Miranda found herself hoping impishly that it wasn't only her mind which was of such keen interest to males, most importantly to Lionel. She hated being indifferent or off-putting to Mr. Upchurch, considering how courteous he had been in the face of social adversity.

"I could understand it if after what has happened you suddenly become terribly busy," she said, offering him a chance to avoid the payment of any further attention to her.

"I appreciate the motive behind what you say." Mr. Upchurch spoke fervently, hand stealing to his heart in an unmistakable sign of utter sincerity, "but permit me to assure you—"

The terms of Mr. Upchurch's reassurance were to remain shrouded in mystery. From the other side of the square an interruption manifested itself.

"I say!" A new voice hailed her. "Miss Powell!"

A young man was rushing toward her. The dark brown eyes and ready smile identified Mr. Oswald Badger. Despite the maze of last night's professed admirers, Mr. Badger's cheery wit had somehow made even his features memorable.

"It is I, your most humble obedient," he began, saluting a female with the sort of words which others used in farewells. He suddenly turned his head with such surprise that the fawn-cloth sports cap on his head seemed to have started in surprise as well. "Aubrey! What could you be doing here?"

"I can't imagine that you haven't already guessed," Aubrey Upchurch answered. The sun sought him out, giving him a look of magisterial propriety suitable to a future Master of Balliol. "No doubt you'll pardon Miss Powell, who you seem to know slightly."

"Know her? My dear fellow, we are meeting here. Miranda ventured forth especially to meet me."

"You and four others, of whom I am one. Miss Powell asked several suitable men to join her."

"Did she indeed?" Oswald Badger threw back his head and

laughed. Such genuine amusement could never have been shared by Aubrey Upchurch or the departed victims of her small hoax. "Beware the female who is out of her native habitat, for she will adapt more swiftly to new surroundings than the mere male."

"Au revoir, Oswald," said Mr. Upchurch with punctilio that even Miranda expected from him by this time.

Mr. Badger, to be sure, continued speaking brightly. "I am very much pleased that a man of academic wisdom is in the supporting cast for my courtship of Miss Powell. I feel certain that she, too, is pleased."

So saying, he moved to Miranda's right side, putting him further from the possible depredations of passing carriage horses and the mud that might rise from the gutters as vehicles hurried along. Mr. Upchurch, of course, had vigilantly positioned himself in the correct manner.

"I strongly disapprove of your manners at this time," Aubrey Upchurch began, hardly offering a thunderbolt to stagger anyone.

Miranda regretted that the well-mannered Mr. Upchurch's feelings were ruffled but found herself amused by the amiable conversation of the heedless Oswald Badger. This conflict would be useful, as she immediately realized, offering her the chance to disaffiliate herself from both ardent swains.

"Gentlemen," she said, looking severely from one to the other, "I have not come here to see you both engage in battle for my affections. Indeed I would look with permanent disfavor upon any such eruption at Covent Garden or in any other outpost of civilization."

"Fisticuffs? I? Never again." Oswald shook his head firmly. "I haven't sported my tens since childhood, and then it was over a slur which someone had made upon a female relative of mine. I regret to say that the slur was correct, and my certainty about the unjustness of the cause I espoused may help to explain why I was soundly thrashed upon that occasion. However, the whole kerfuffle has bred in me a detestation of fisticuffs, and it persists to this moment."

Aubrey Upchurch responded by drawing out a hand for the

other to take as a sign that a bond had been pledged. Oswald, of course, didn't see the gesture made by someone whose responses were not of the greatest moment.

"Now that agreement has been reached," Miranda said as Oswald belatedly accepted the token without his eyes leaving Miranda's face, "I feel sure that you will both pardon me for leaving so early."

Protests could be heard as she walked half a dozen yards to where the patient Mrs. Saltfield was standing. The older woman seemed reluctant to call for a hansom and escort Miranda from the presence of two eligible prospective husbands, each of whom was keenly interested in her.

Miranda didn't share that reluctance to any degree. She hailed a hansom and gave the address in Jermyn Street as her destination and that of her chopfallen companion. She couldn't help feeling convinced that neither man would call upon her again. In different ways she felt unhappy about not seeing one or the other as a possible suitor. What mattered, however, was that her problem with these men was now solved, and she was free to concentrate her wiles upon Lionel and none other.

Beyond peradventure of doubt, she repeated to herself in the hope of imparting conviction to her sensibilities, the problem was solved.

It may be considered fortunate that Miranda couldn't guess at the feelings of both men after she left them.

Aubrey, breathing heavily at the recent contact with divinity, felt for the first time that Miranda Powell was a truly magnificent young woman with whom to consider spending the years to come in a state of marriage. Wise, witty, most attractive, and supremely adaptable. No man in his position would want much more from a wife. He could imagine the pleasure of introducing her to the life of a university! How eagerly she would learn what he alone would be in a position to teach her!

Oswald, in his own view, found Miss Powell very likeable indeed, but nothing more. It was beyond his powers to know why Aubrey, a fortunate young man who had made peace with the world of economics, would favor Miss Powell over the likes of a wonderful girl like Charlotte Dempster.

Oswald turned away before Aubrey, who remained looking after the departing hansom. He didn't say a word in farewell. For once he was dispirited. He couldn't possibly feel otherwise after having been confronted with the knowledge that he had a rival for the hand of a girl he didn't really want to marry.

In a way that he failed to completely understand, the situation was galling and irritating and mildly humorous as well. But he was the butt of the humor this time, and it wasn't a position that Oswald Badger could bring himself to appreciate.

CHAPTER TEN

Another Game Is Afoot

Lionel was returning to his seat at Lord's to watch the afternoon play. He had found himself on the premier cricket ground in Britain because a visit to the Duke of Harranmuir had concluded with the Duke's wish to see his son play for the Marylebone Club. Ever agreeable to cosseting an influential politico, Lionel had accompanied Harranmuir out to Maida Vale.

The game was well under way as he advanced on the seats, wickets having been pitched at eleven. An hour's adjournment lay ahead at two, and stumps would finally be drawn at six or thereabouts. Lionel, who hadn't played the national game since early manhood, had seen the Zingerees eleven on the pitch at Kennington Oval a year ago. Privately he hoped that the Zingerees would emerge victorious over the M.C.C., but it wasn't a desire he would have expressed to Harranmuir, not by any means.

Players were shifting from one end of the pitch to the other, causing witnesses to the match to stir restlessly. Just as he was turning, Lionel heard his name called.

His first gentlemanly impulse was to glance along the row to where Charlotte waited for him. Having known Miss Dempster since their gilded youth, he was well aware that she was mildly impatient at watching a game like this, probably because amateurs and gentlemen were pitted against each other. He caught her eye, postponing his return with a gesture, then looked back of him to the row he had just passed.

A bright-haired and gray-eyed young man was rising from

one of the seats and approaching the aisle space. There was room for a quiet conversation.

"Your Lordship, I have just come from a few moments with Miss Powell, your ward," said Aubrey Upchurch. "I consider myself most fortunate to have encountered you here."

Lionel's attention was drawn away from a bye on the field, the ball having passed the wicket without being touched. "I saw Miss Powell myself only this morning, and I assume that she remains in good health over the few hours that have passed."

"Your Lordship, I must tell you that I am deeply impressed with Miss Miranda."

Lionel's eyes narrowed as he considered this stop-press news. Aubrey Upchurch, belatedly identified, was one of those who had requested a dance with Miranda at the Marmonts' ball on the preceding night. The son of a wealthy railroad man, he was probably showing disdain for his father by cloistering himself in a university. It was distracting to hear of a dry stick like Aubrey Upchurch taking the slightest notice of a female rather than some textbook in Latin.

"Miss Miranda is so—so educable," the lothario proceeded, not entirely surprising Lionel by this time. "One wants to see her eyes widen in pleasure as she learns of this or that."

The question had, of course, been answered. Aubrey Upchurch apparently saw Miranda as someone to be taught rather than loved or cherished. Lionel didn't appreciate the degree of scorn that coursed through him. Sir Francis Upchurch, to name only one picaro of industry, would never have admired a young female because her knowledge could be strengthened. It made Lionel wonder that such a father could have helped spawn so dismal a creature.

"I don't know that my ward has any Greek or other languages, and I believe her acquaintance with the sciences is only minimal," Lionel said, responding as best he could to the other's farrago. "I certainly envy her teacher the vast field that would open up to him."

His attention strayed once more. There was a lively discussion nearby as to whether the bowler's foot had been in the crease at a strategic time, an inquiry to which Lionel would rather have given his attention.

"I was not thinking to offer Miss Miranda instruction in any academic area, certainly not at this time," Aubrey confessed hurriedly. He was a good-mannered young man, but even courtesy had to give way at some time to the needs of communicating.

Lionel's attention returned to him with gratifying speed.

"I am hoping to call upon her," Aubrey said, causing Lionel to forget some of his scorn. Aubrey looked directly into the Earl's eyes, following the same mode of frank and fearless behavior as was advocated for an Englishman confronting a tiger or other unsophisticated beast.

"I see." Lionel nodded in comprehension.

"Please accept my assurances, sir," said Aubrey Upchurch needlessly, "that my intentions are entirely honorable."

Lionel would have been dumbfounded if Mr. Upchurch was capable of any other intention. Although he had just shown himself possessed by human feelings, in however distorted a guise, Lionel's opinion of him had plummeted again.

Some response had to be made quickly. Lionel certainly knew that Oswald Badger was considered the most likely of candidates for his ward's hand, but it was undiplomatic to let another be turned down while the matter remained undecided. The quality of the suitor was not to any point. Aubrey Upchurch might be far from stimulating, and his idea of intense pleasure would probably have catapulted any young girl into a long sleep. Nonetheless it was not wise to burnish grievances against him.

"I will take the matter under my most earnest advisement and keep you informed," he said finally.

"Thank you, Your Lordship," Aubrey beamed. "A prospective suitor could ask no more."

Lionel didn't correct him.

By the time he resumed the journey to his place in the stands, a ball on the field had given an unexpected bound and was promptly buttered on a fieldsman's leg side. There was a commiserating groan from the attentive audience just as Lionel settled down next to his affianced.

Lionel was so deep in thought that he didn't make another remark about the extraordinary effect of rose poplin upon Miss Dempster's figure, as he had enthusiastically done earlier.

"How did Harranmuir's son perform?" he asked immediately.

"Oh yes, young Edward you mean." Charlotte looked regretful. "I noticed at the time, Lionel dear, but I have forgotten since."

The tenth Marylebone batsman had just been dismissed, requiring another pause. Lionel used the time, without an apology to Charlotte, for drawing the necessary information from a neighbor. As a result he knew that upon encountering the Duke at the adjournment it would be necessary to sympathize rather than offer congratulations.

Charlotte had occupied most of the game time in wondering how much progress Oswald was making with Miranda. During the last minute or two, however, she had been restless.

"What did Aubrey Upchurch want from you?" she asked. Aubrey had attended last night's ball, and it seemed to her that any difficulty concerning him and Lionel would have been bruited at that time. Unless something new had come up, she told herself, and the popular Miranda was involved.

If Lionel had not been in the company of a female, and especially his affianced, he would have snorted. "Aubrey Upchurch wants permission to call upon Miranda with a view, as he gives me to understand, of eventual marriage."

"Might I ask how you responded?"

"Diplomatically. I told him that the matter will be taken under advisement."

"With what result? Lionel dear, let us not fence about this."

"I can see no harm in permitting him to call," Lionel said. "It would be impossible to tell you how strongly I disapprove of any marriage between such opposites, but the overwhelming consideration for us and my career is that of getting Miranda married off, I fear."

Charlotte's objection was of a different nature altogether. It seemed to her that if none other than Oswald Badger offered on the horizon, Miranda must be more inclined to accept him without making heavy weather. It was impossible for Charlotte to imagine that in any choice between the two men Oswald wouldn't be favored, but women's tastes, as some poet must have caterwauled over the years, can be variable.

"Yes, Aubrey Upchurch would make an unimpressive husband to a girl like Miranda."

"Unimpressive, but upon thinking it over I realize that he is palpably respectable. For that reason, my dear, he can be useful."

"Your attitude has changed, it seems."

"I recognize reality."

Charlotte suspected that he had actually recognized something else. Aubrey Upchurch was certain to seem so unlikely a husband that Miranda couldn't possibly accept him, which would leave her free. Tortuous reasoning, perhaps, but not for a diplomat or his affianced.

"Don't you want to see Miranda married to someone you can be proud to show off in society?"

"Of course, but I don't feel that Aubrey is a social liability."

It seemed to Charlotte that he was working hard to convince himself accordingly.

"I would truly advise you to let well enough alone. Oswald can be brought to make an offer for Miranda, I feel certain, and he is a young man who would make any female happy."

She didn't think he could have detected a certain quaver she had been unable to keep from putting into her voice.

"Happy, yes, but he must needs be financed," Lionel said crossly. "He would be a continual drain on a guardian-at-law. You cannot deny that."

"Even a mild drain on an ample income is better than condemning a young woman to perpetual unhappiness, to a life where she has to pretend that she is ill simply in order to get through a day. Eventually she does become ill along the lines that she has wished upon herself. You know of several such instances and so do I."

Charlotte didn't add that her mother's was a different example altogether, as she perpetually quarreled with her spouse as the only way in which she could bring herself to communicate with him. The thought of her parents recalled why she was plumping so vigorously for Oswald Badger to succeed in marrying another female and thereby clear the way for her to wed dear Lionel and keep the elders in comfort forever afterwards.

"Oswald Badger is very fine," she added. "A man who happens to be both good-tempered and witty."

The quaver in her tones was far more noticeable this time. Lionel responded quickly. "You seem unusually fond of him."

"Indeed I am, and I don't want to see Oswald or Miranda being unhappy for life."

Lionel's look was brief. Satisfied that she had been truthful, as expected, he turned away without putting the question that had occurred unbidden to him.

On the field, one of the Zingerees had bowled his five before the over, and there was a spatter of applause. Lionel joined heartily.

Charlotte was making a mental note of the increased necessity to let Oswald know that he had to obtain the speediest possible results in his wooing.

More than ever, there was not a moment to be lost.

CHAPTER ELEVEN

Two Talks Against Time

Her most humble obedient, as Charlotte occasionally thought of
Oswald, happened to be one of the guests at the Duke and
Duchess of Harranmuir's supper party that night in their town
house on Davies Street. Oswald was a friend of the Duke's
youngest son, not the cricketer, and this latter had particularly
asked for Mr. Badger to be invited.

Charlotte, who was attending with Lionel, had been unable
to corner Oswald for a brief conversation. Perhaps she was
flattering herself, but it seemed that the males were going out of
their way to find opportunities for engaging her in conversation. More than likely a contributing factor was the azure gown
she was wearing, with its open bodice. Nothing more provoca-
tive was being shown than the lace front, but men always
seemed to be hopeful that there had been some perceptible
error in design on the part of the modiste and that it must be
possible to see more if only one was close enough.

Forty guests trooped into the dining room at eight o'clock.
Chinese lanterns, suspended from the dark blue ceiling, created a pleasant gleam. Places had been set and distances mea-
sured meticulously. At the left in every setting, with prongs up,
were the Three Graces, as Charlotte referred to forks for salad,
meat, and fish. Knives for meat and fish appeared on the right,
edges toward the plate. Soup spoon and oyster fork had been
eased into their proper places. No doubt some added utensils
would be needed during the Lucullan festival which was getting under way.

Oswald didn't have an opportunity to ingratiate himself with

Lionel until the latter's burgundy had been poured and the butler was retreating behind the Duchess's chair to oversee the service.

"I am truly envious of you, Your Lordship," Oswald said at that juncture.

Lionel, made querulous by an overture from this source but admirably attempting to hide his feelings, spoke after a pause.

"How so, sir?"

"Because you see Miranda every day, you talk to her and often dine with her."

As bad luck would have it, Oswald was seated too far off for Charlotte to urge discretion upon him. Talking about Miranda at this large dinner was more than enough, in Lionel's particular situation, to put his back up.

The Duke, overhearing, chuckled. He was a handsome man with muttonchop whiskers. "Surely not a lady friend, Lionel."

"By no means, I assure you."

Charlotte attempted to signal Oswald that the time had come to draw it mild. Oswald's eyes were swiveling around toward the head of the table, however, and he was too far off for a swift under-the-table kick to reach him.

Oswald said, "I was referring, sir, to the Earl's ward."

Charlotte interjected a little loudly just as the clear soup was being taken away, "A sweet child indeed."

Oswald had turned back to Lionel now, anxious to see how favorable an impression he might be making as a prospective suitor. In that guise, he blandly contradicted Charlotte.

"Miss Miranda is far from a child, if I may be permitted to say so, far from it."

Charlotte spoke as the mutton haunch was being trundled out. "A female becomes older so soon that she looks different to various observers."

That sentiment was sufficiently vague as to draw wise nods from most of the assemblage.

The Duchess, from her end of the table, put in owlishly, "I detect that we are not being taken into the confidence of every speaker."

At this moment, the wife of Mr. Benjamin Disraeli whispered

soothingly, and the Duchess relapsed into that state of coiled quiet which characterized her public persona at most times.

Lionel quickly brought the subject around to a consideration of the quality of Mr. Holman Hunt's outdoor paintings. It sufficed as a distraction through the entree, which consisted of a fish that had apparently been flayed alive. With this concoction a great quantity of scalded vegetables were served. The time given for digesting the sorbet was devoted to a consideration of the chances that Parliament might pass an antibribery act. Over the steaming and welcome oolong, Mr. Disraeli imperceptibly led a discussion about the future of Tasmania. The moment that Charlotte gathered it was a convict colony that had been named, some auditor insisted that the subject was far too delicate for consideration in mixed company.

By that time, Charlotte had been able to catch Oswald's eyes. So well did these two understand each other that only a look was needed before he realized that he had gone too far a while ago. By use of similar necromancy, she conveyed additionally that she was desirous of a private conversation with him.

That wish wasn't granted until long after the ladies had retired to discuss the raising of children, the agonies of dealing with servants, and such other matters as came into their purview. Charlotte saw him in the huge drawing room, the gentlemen having consumed port and sherry and claret before joining their ladies. Lionel was already involved in a discussion with a Scottish peer whose name seemed to consist exclusively of glottal stops. Oswald, having tactfully divested himself of an enamored baroness whose husband had imbibed too freely, suggested that they seek out an unoccupied corner.

"Until now, I had always thought that you were skillful at getting onto the good side of someone with influence and money." It was a brisk greeting, as she was well aware, but the mood for niceties had passed.

"Your affianced simply doesn't like me no matter what I do." Oswald somehow excused himself without seeming plaintive. "If I was able to stand on my head and keep balance with one finger, he would snarl about that finger."

"Recalling the use to which you put your head a while ago, I wouldn't concur that there was anything to be protected," Charlotte remarked. "It's not as if you were being offered a chance to hitch up your lot with one of the sisters in Macbeth."

"No, of course not. I like Miranda, word on it! She's fresh, eager, generous of nature."

He paused by way of indicating that there was one drawback he wouldn't name and saw no way to overcome.

Charlotte knew perfectly well what he was referring to, but ignored the obvious. If she flushed in near embarrassment, she couldn't see it in her own face.

"Your need for money is almost as great as mine," she said, and though it didn't seem possible for her to speak more quietly she managed it now. "You are certainly au courant with both situations, and it is unnecessary to review matters for your benefit."

"Indeed it is, my dear Charlotte."

It was the particular intimacy of that interpolated phrase, so similar to Lionel's form of address for her, that played hob with Charlotte's temper.

"I am limiting our converse to the major item on the agenda, so to speak, and that involves your courtship of Miranda." A deep breath coursed through Charlotte's body, calming her to a certain extent. "There is a rival for Miranda's hand, not to say for the balance of that young lady."

"Aubrey Upchurch, you mean? I have seen that demon lover in talk with the object of his affections." Oswald shrugged, vouchsafing no clarification of the circumstances. "And what chance could he possibly have against me in such a contest? None at all, my dear Charlotte. You know it perfectly."

This time she winced. "The object of the current exercise, Oswald, is for me to inform you an even greater need now exists for you to act quickly."

"I appreciate the bulletin and can assure you that I am already doing so."

"Have you planned on a proposal to be made tomorrow morning?"

"Of course not. That would be far too crude."

"It is not romantic, I agree. Moonlight and a long walk are

romantic. Then a male should turn his young woman to face him and look deep into her eyes and speak in a thrilling voice. That approach would be without exception. But there is no time for delicacies of such an order."

"No time?" Oswald was startled once more. "I can now almost certainly assure you that Miranda would not ever permit herself to get into a condition which requires the balm of instant marriage."

"What you say there is true in its more gross aspect, but you must have realized during the recent feast that Lionel cannot afford to spend much more time with a nubile ward under his roof. It would hurt his career beyond retrieval for many, many years." She chose not to add that her chances of a financially advantageous marriage to a man of whom she was rather fond could be decimated as a direct result.

"Tomorrow morning, eh?"

"I will inform my affianced that you intend to manifest yourself in Jermyn Street at ten o'clock in the morning."

"Not ten," he protested. "I would have to rise at eight simply to prepare myself."

"Let us say at eleven, then. Not a moment past that, however. Lionel departs for the day shortly afterwards, as a rule, and I want him nearby to give his imprimatur to the arrangement almost immediately."

"If a cleric is nearby as well, perhaps hiding in the next room, I can marry Miranda Powell without further ado."

"Would that it might be arranged in just such a fashion!"

Oswald drew back, examining Charlotte's neoclassic features almost as if for the first time.

"You don't really mean that."

"I will make it a point to be at Jermyn Street when you arrive," Charlotte said distantly. "And now perhaps you will pardon me. Dear Lionel is on the horizon, so to speak, and will be escorting me back to the bosom of my family."

Faustine Saltfield, although respectable to the fingertips, was a lady with a minor vice. In many circles it would have been considered a pleasant addiction. She drew contentment from

attending a music hall. No one would have admitted more
quickly that her fancy was a lower-class amusement, by and
large. Often, though, she found identification with sentiments
expressed by various mummers, and it gave her a thrill that she
didn't obtain in cheap novels or sanctimonious journals.

She could never know in advance when it would be possible
to get away from the various obligations and random delights of
her position in Lionel's household. On this evening, however,
Lionel had escorted Charlotte to supper, and Miranda had
promptly gone to bed without nourishment. It was an ideal
time to indulge her once-a-month pleasure.

For this expedition she dressed in light blue with a flurry of
braiding. As it wasn't a combination she normally favored, it
served as a disguise of sorts, although she hardly felt like
Haroun-al-Raschid venturing forth to the alleyways of Baghdad.

A hansom took her along the cool streets out to Astley's establishment off Bruton Street and hard by Piccadilly. At the pay
box she learned to her dismay that none but gallery seats were
available for tonight's performance at this palace of varieties. In
the circumstances, she purchased one.

Not till she was on her way up the zigzag staircase did she
become aware of a well-dressed man walking behind her. He
wore black, with a slightly pointed collar and stringpiece tie.
Probably in the early fifties, he was tall and nicely knit, with a
sailor's walk. It was a mystery that a man who had probably
been exposed to scant food and the youthful sicknesses of poor
folk had grown tall and handsome.

Faustine Saltfield was not at all impressed by the lower classes
who made up the bulk of the audience. Shirts had been put on
the railing, and more than one man was wearing cross-braces
over a bare chest while waiting for the entertainment to get
under way. Babies admitted at half price were squalling at the
sight of grimy-faced sweeps and pale dustmen, the latter seeking momentary relief from hard lives with the aid of pleasant
melodies and vivid tableaus. Certainly she was being offered a
glimpse of the sad and sordid London that was cheek-by-jowl
with the City of the quality, but it was knowledge she could well
have prospered without acquiring.

It seemed to her a fortunate circumstance that the well-dressed man took a seat close to hers. His glance ranged in her direction, and she thought it just as well to sit beside him. Removing her bonnet after she had seated herself was enough to give some needed play to her darkened hair.

"The pleasures of the poor," he said quietly to her.

She had in fact been enjoying the sight of the music hall's interior, with its white and lemon and green and gold, as well as those crimson hangings from the shilling boxes. At his remark, she felt decidedly unsettled.

"It surprises me, ma'am, that someone dressed like yourself would come up to sit here."

She made an exception to her lifelong rule of never speaking to strangers. After all, he had shown courtesy and was well dressed, softly spoken, and decidedly handsome for an older man.

"No other location was available."

She struggled to think of something else to say. Years had passed since she had involved herself in casual conversation with daring males, and she envied Miranda Powell's talent for bringing it off gaily.

He looked pleased at the sound of her voice, which was in itself decidedly gratifying. It didn't occur to Mrs. Saltfield that he was a little taken aback by her in turn, and for that reason he spoke more directly now.

"You are Mrs. Faustine Saltfield, of course," said this amazing stranger.

From that moment, if only for his having spoken her name in a public place, it would be impossible to think of him as a gentleman.

"I have come to witness a performance, not to engage in idle chatter."

He nodded as if she had calmly agreed with his statement. "My name is Roland Travit, and I—"

Whatever else he was going to say was drowned out by sounds of the gallery members whistling and catcalling. Somebody threw an orange peel toward the boxes, but it landed down in the sixpenny seats. Nutshells were directed at the gold curtain.

The orchestra at the back of the stage began to play a popular tune.

". . . followed you to this place," Mr. Travit was saying at her left ear, his words audible in spite of the music. "I had come to the house in Jermyn Street and hoped to speak with the Earl, but was unable to get past that butler who smiles continually while declining to do what you ask."

An apt portrait in words of the majordomo, Grimm, and proof that the infernal Travit had been in contact with at least one other member of Lionel's establishment.

"I waited close to the house in confidence that the Earl would appear," Mr. Travit continued. "He did show himself with a young lady and both climbed into what I feel certain must be his brougham. Running toward his lordship and shouting was not enough to draw his attention as the departure came so quickly."

She wanted to ask the reason for his efforts and before obtaining an answer to make a scene. How gratifying it would be to chastise this upstart with a gloved palm and leave immediately! But every lower-class stranger in the gallery would suddenly be aware of her. More important, she would not have learned what she now felt she had to know.

"I don't doubt that you are curious to discover what information is of such a character that your comments would be as useful as his lordship's."

That difficulty would be resolved soon enough, and she was at least prepared to make a show of disinterest. It seemed more ladylike and offered time to still the sudden beating of her heart. Instinct told her of the possible usefulness in showing a gentlewoman's sangfroid to this admittedly handsome rascal.

She made a point of shifting her head to the right, hoping to be out of his earshot. The remedy might not have been efficacious, considering how clearly he was able to speak, but the entertainment began at last and caused additional sounds to overwhelm even Roland Travit's crystal-clear enunciation.

Dancers were applauded vigorously in the gallery, and a tableau was at least tolerated. At long last Mr. Percy Pennymore, the illustrious comic singer, appeared with some new offerings. Shrewdly he persuaded the entire audience to join him at the first reprised stanza of his first selection. To the accompaniment of vigorous applause the ditty was again repeated, but so cleverly that most of the audience members felt that they had helped compose it and were proud of their collective musicality and wit.

During the last repetition, heads were swaying in time to the melody, which dealt with a paucity of snow to be expected at Christmas. Mr. Travit was prepared for the moment when Mrs. Saltfield's head was closer to his.

". . . adopted a girl . . ." were the words on which he put the greatest emphasis.

They had been well chosen if his intent was that of riveting her attention. Mrs. Saltfield's voice explored a note that she could not possibly have intended to reach, and she whirled on the loathsome stranger. Her demeanor was as forbidding as she could make it.

"What did you say?"

"I asked whether it is true that your nephew, the Earl of Wingham, has adopted a girl who is (how did I put it?) of an age."

Her mind was working quickly. If this odious man had followed her in order to ask that one question he must have had an urgent reason for doing so. Obviously he was not an official to whom the truth, if not the nature of the misunderstanding on hers and Lionel's part, must be known. He was therefore an employee of one of those gossip newspapers with which London was dotted nowadays, organs intended to communicate scandals among society people and bring that knowledge to the attention of denizens in the lower class.

It would be idle to pretend that Mrs. Saltfield hadn't occasionally encountered one of these newspapers and even held it in a hand. In order to identify the object for what it actually was, she had absorbed its contents. Without approving of the material, as no well-raised female could do, it was an occasional relief to see something besides the sanctimonious pseudo-uplifting journals which were on sale in so many places. Like her dearly beloved Joseph, the soldier who had fathered Miranda Powell with another woman, Mrs. Saltfield felt only a slight tolerance for all officially approved attitudes. On occasion she had chuckled quietly to think of the discomfiture of some peer or politician when a peccadillo of his private life was broadly hinted at.

Never could she have expected a difficulty along those lines to involve her nephew. Certainly not as the result of a series of accidents such as had brought Miranda to find a home in Jermyn Street if only on the most temporary basis. It would be impossible to offer the least explanation to some lickspittle like this one who defiled Faustine Saltfield by sitting next to her.

It happened that Mr. Percy Pennymore, that popular singer of comic songs, chose this moment for a retreat from the scene of his recent triumph, no doubt in hopes of being urged by applause to come out again. A dustman started to jeer Mr. Pennymore, and another dustman attacked his colleague. Several able-bodied men cheered both combatants on, rather than halting the *guerre à outrance* that was proceeding in their immediate vicinity.

Amid the distraction, it would have been possible for Mrs. Saltfield to leave unobserved. She stood, hurried to the end of the aisle, and rushed to the exits. She was aware of Mr. Travit rising with the likely plan of following her. The battlers, moving around this gallery level with undiminished vigor, fell up against Mr. Travit as he stirred, nearly pitching him over the rail and into one of the more expensive accommodations.

He called out with dismay. A toothless crone, her sympathies stirred by the sight of a handsome gentleman in difficulty, approached the men, pulled them apart, administered a severe tongue lashing, and emphasized her disapproval by knocking their heads together.

Mrs. Saltfield was already halfway down the zigzag stairs and then out onto the bustling street. There was news of great import to give Lionel and little time to be lost.

CHAPTER TWELVE

The Wrong Offer Is Finally Made

"Please ask Miss Miranda if she will be good enough to join me," said his lordship.

The butler left in order to demand that one of the maids do the Earl's bidding. Lionel began pacing the large sitting room on the lower floor of his home. Plans had already been made, and it was now necessary to put them into action.

Only a clod would have failed to recognize the ever-increasing necessity of acting in the matter of Miranda Powell's future. His aunt had waited up for him last night and told him about the incident at Astley's Music Hall Theatre. At least one journalist now scented the possibility of a scandal that would sell copies of some infernal penny-sheet! Charlotte had informed him that she would be paying a visit to Jermyn Street later this morning, and so would Oswald Badger. It was distinctly possible, she added, that the impatient Badger would immediately make an offer for Miranda in marriage.

An offer and its immediate acceptance would resolve all the difficulties that had been plaguing him these last days, permitting his career to proceed and his marriage to take place. It was also true that Charlotte's improvident father, who had plunged his family's money into such unlikely investments as a print telegraph and a form of steel that would be suitable for boiler plating in the unlikely event that it could ever be perfected, would at last be provided for. Charlotte, too, would be happier. There was, after all, nothing wrong with marriage to a female one had known from childhood, a female with whom one was entirely at ease. Indeed there was nothing wrong for him in making a marriage to a dear girl like Charlotte Dempster. Nothing at all.

What remained now was for him to speak with Miranda and make it wholly clear that if Oswald Badger introduced the subject of possible marriage between them, she was to agree with all maidenly haste. Suddenly aware that he felt weak in the direction of his kneecaps, a disconcerting response from a former member of the Leander Rowing Club, Lionel sat down abruptly in hopes of controlling the quavers. It was almost sufficient.

Miranda came hurtling down the stairs but paused before the large sitting room. Listening to the steps and the halt, Lionel knew that she was smoothing her dress at the last minute. On any other occasion he would have smiled.

It didn't seem as if any repair could have been necessary when she finally materialized. Miranda wore a new merino day dress in lavender. The center part in her flaming red hair was delightfully irregular, as if it had been affectionately rumpled by someone else's hand. Looking away on the instant, he met her forest-green eyes, sparkling at the sight of him. He told himself disparagingly that she had been using kohl on her brows to give the eyes a particular reflected gleam, as he understood many females did, but that explanation seemed inadequate.

"Here you are," he began, stating the obvious in so glum a tone that her eyes clouded over. "You have been informed by my aunt that you are to expect a particular visitor this morning."

"Mr. Badger, yes." Miranda spoke calmly. She was expecting to hear a denunciation of the witty Oswald. In the time-honored tradition of woman as she understood it, she imagined herself serving as a mediator between opposing males.

"Doubtless you know what Mr. Badger will want."

"Yes, it was made clear to me." She spoke more calmly than she had expected. His own flat tone had caused a ghastly thought to enter her brain. Despite everything that had taken place between them, was he actually going to throw her away after all, to cast her into outer darkness?

"Mr. Badger is likely to suggest that you marry him."

Lionel looked down at his hands, which were folding and unfolding in his lap. He didn't feel surprised by any means that two men had expressed an interest in her. It was a source of wonder to him that all of London's young men weren't at her feet.

Miranda couldn't have been aware that his thoughts were taking that particular turn. Nor would she have found much to console her in the particular evidence of his regard.

"I feel certain that you intend to be a good girl and do so. I cannot conceive that someone like you, Miranda, would act against the wishes of those who are concerned to guide you in life, who are older and wiser, and who think and act with the consideration of what will be best for your future."

Lionel would have felt no resentment whatever if a bolt of lightning had suddenly appeared and struck him dead. Having survived, however, the quacksalver proceeded.

"I know that you have formed a splendid opinion of so worthwhile a gentleman as Mr. Badger."

"I appreciate him as a companion for a dance or a conversation."

Lionel wished in turn that Miranda could have managed two notes in her speaking voice. That was a reaction which Charlotte or even his Aunt Saltfield would have anticipated and consequently produced an array of sounds no matter what their actual feelings. Miranda, incapable of dissimulation in a serious matter, sounded as if she had been numbed.

"Then I take it that the outcome is virtually settled." Sympathetically he added, " 'Pon my word, I wish that you didn't have to be badgered."

Only when he saw the sudden smile on Miranda's full lips was he aware that her quick imagination had given the observation a humorous cast. With all his will he ordered himself not to smile, as this matter was far too serious for levity of any stripe whatever. But his own practicality kept him from denying the humor that she had discovered. Eyes met, and they were smiling freely at each other.

He knew he was going to laugh but stood abruptly, as if that movement would cause him to stop himself. Warningly, for the dancing-eyed Miranda's benefit, he put a forefinger to his lips to impose silence on her. In impish mimicry, she did the same. The actions, as each ought to have anticipated, now represented a fresh source of humor.

Moving back and forth to help contain themselves, they shook in laughter that Lionel didn't want anyone else to hear. The necessity for silence, of course, was a further prod upon the risibilities. Miranda suddenly reached out for him, and he accepted her, enfolding her waist in one arm and then joining the other to circle her more tightly.

They were involved in this activity, still unable to stop their silent laughter, when the door opened with alarming suddenness and Charlotte Dempster walked into the room.

Lionel's first thought, unworthy though it might be, was simply that Charlotte was making too much of a habit of sudden entrances in his home. On this occasion she hadn't even permitted Grimm to announce her. It did seem as if she was taking entirely too much upon herself by moving around the place as if she were its chatelaine.

Of course he kept the thoughts to himself. Disdaining the pretense that he had been comforting Miranda through an unseemly display of emotion, he released her without another word. Miranda turned away, drawing deep breaths to suppress the cascade of silent laughter. More than once she reminded herself that a woman of whom she was fond would be gravely affronted by the sight that had met her eyes.

Charlotte Dempster, however, was speaking calmly to Lionel when Miranda finally turned back. No doubt she had decided to take a pacific view of the brief episode she had partly witnessed, a diplomatic gesture worthy of Lionel in the throes of his vocation. Miranda appreciated it for all their sakes.

"Mr. Badger arrived only a moment after I did," Charlotte was saying, "and wants to speak with Miranda."

Oswald might indeed have been discerned in the outer hall, where Grimm had directed that he stand. For this notable occasion Oswald was dressed in one of his few remaining worthy rigouts: a morning coat with sloped front, turned-down collar, and loosely knitted tie, plaid trousers, and lace-up pitch-black shoes. Ruefully he told himself that he was in full fig for proposing marriage to a girl he liked but didn't love.

Grimm came into view once again after several minutes. Deferentially he suggested that Mr. Badger find his way to the large sitting room. As an aid in reaching this goal, Grimm gestured toward the proper direction and even indicated the correct door.

On his way, Oswald was aware of footsteps hurrying up one of the stairs and out of his sight. A bulldog growled when he knocked, but one moment's reflection convinced him that the master of this establishment had been directing him to open the door.

Inside he did discover a petulant bulldog, causing him to consider the merits of a swift departure. Charlotte was in the room as well, however, her eyes gravely inspecting both her white-gloved hands. She didn't seem aware that he was among those present. Mrs. Saltfield, the Earl's aunt, was looking out the large window and saying impatiently, "I see no sign of him now, thank heavens." Those words were somewhat mysterious to anyone ignorant of the existence of Mr. Roland Travit and caused Oswald to consider that no one in the room but himself seemed to have the slightest idea that anyone else was present.

There was a commotion from the softest chair, and the Earl rose from its depths. Dutifully he was affixing a smile to his lips, a sight which caused Oswald to remain.

"I understand that you are desirous of speaking to my ward," the Earl said in what was intended to be a pleasant manner.

"That's correct, Your Lordship."

Wingham growled, causing the bulldog to look up enviously.

It was Charlotte, without altering the angle of her head, who contributed the information it was vital for the suitor to obtain at this juncture.

"Miranda is in the small sitting room upstairs," she said so quietly that it wasn't easy to detect the words. "I am certain that Mrs. Saltfield would be happy to escort you there."

The aunt stirred and turned. Her smile was more enthusiastic by far than that of the Earl. Oswald couldn't help feeling at least mildly gratified by the reminder that females in varying stages of dissolution found him a noteworthy addition to their list of acquaintances.

"Please follow me, Mr. Badger," the aunt said. On the carpeted steps in the hallway, feeling the necessity to impede thought by conversation, she added, "The dear girl is terribly nervous, terribly excited at the prospect of your calling upon her."

"Ah." He felt that way himself and could sympathize to the fullest.

"From the moment she met you, Mr. Badger, Miranda has been unable to talk of anyone else. I have heard almost no name on her lips but yours since the Marmonts' ball."

With his habitual courtesy, Oswald forebore to point out that Miranda's having arranged a rendezvous with five men on the next afternoon was certainly a curious method for indicating that a powerful impression had been made on her. Possibly, though, she had wanted to convey that she, too, could develop a coterie of admirers. Despite the many good points that have been noted in his character, he couldn't help being more than a little vain about his previous successes with the fair sex.

Panting slightly from her exertions up the carpeted stairs, Mrs. Saltfield continued, "And I can truly tell you that Miranda is a wonderful girl, sweet, fresh, affectionate, and respectful. The man she accepts for a husband will be truly among the blessed."

From the top of the stairs, Mrs. Saltfield approached the nearest door, knocked twice, and opened it without an invitation.

"He is here," she said without further clarification and stepped to one side.

Feeling like the tenor in some infernal *opérette*, Oswald walked into the room. He saw instantly that Miranda was sensibly dressed in lavender, which certainly became her. She was looking down at herself almost as Charlotte had been doing downstairs. Except for the perky Mrs. Saltfield, Jermyn Street today appeared to be rife with distrait females.

After noticing that the door had sensibly been left open, Oswald cleared his throat to introduce the topic of his discourse.

In a sudden access of reserve, as his previous relations with the fair sex had not involved discussions of marriage, he adopted a more roundabout approach.

"I—I have something of great import to say to you," he began. It would have been most appealing to sound as if he were deranged by passion, but he suspected that Miranda would see through such a guise. In spite of her tender years, she must have driven many a young male to the brink of distraction.

Miranda wanted to look up and smile, but her feelings made it impossible. Although she was unnerving a man who had done no harm to her at all and who was actually anxious to pay her the greatest compliment that any man could pay a woman, the knowledge changed nothing for her.

"Miranda, you must be aware," he resumed briskly, and then cleared his throat and looked away at the myriad gewgaws and decorations with which this chamber was infested. Politeness alone required him to look directly at the person being addressed, and indeed it presented no difficulty whatever to observe Miranda, except that she seemed so moody.

"You must be aware, as I say, that from the moment I first met you I have been stirred to my depths."

By an effort of will, Miranda did look up. Her eyes seemed glassy.

Oswald was actually grateful for once when this comely girl's eyes returned to a detailed consideration of her gloved hands. He had not thought of Miranda Powell as one of those silent types who wanted a man to make every initiative. Apparently he had been mistaken.

"My feelings for you," he went on, conscious that he was approaching the Rubicon with extensive preparation, "have been deeper and truer than those of mere friendship."

At long last she spoke, her voice coming as if from a great distance.

"I understand."

The fact of speech emanating from Miranda in this mood must be an encouragement in itself, the equivalent, perhaps, of a Spanish señorita making small excited motions with her fan.

"For that reason, Miranda—Miss Powell—Miranda, I have

the honor to ask your hand in marriage. Will you do me the
honor of becoming my wife?"

Miranda had occupied herself in evolving a decision that
would keep her from wounding Oswald's masculine sensibilities. Certainly the die seemed cast and no choice confronted
her any longer, but she didn't want to pronounce the three-
letter word that would seal her fate, that would cause her to
spend a lifetime away from the man she knew she loved.

"I am aware and deeply appreciative of the honor that you
have done me," she murmured, speaking slowly.

As he wanted this particular negotiation concluded on the
instant, Oswald asked, "And you accept with alacrity, I take it?"

She was silent.

"You don't decline?" A pit seemed to have opened under his
feet, disgorging creditors of all ages and sizes. It was an imaginative stroke that Miranda would certainly have admired and
envied.

"It will be necessary for you to speak with my guardian and
obtain his consent."

She was determined to have Lionel approve of his future
unhappiness and hers and do it in the plainest possible words.

"But he *is* in favor of the arrangement, I can assure you."
Oswald knew perfectly well that the Earl may not have been
overjoyed at the prospect of an infusion of Badger into his
family, even the remote family, but his lordship had bowed to
the inevitable. "As a result, then, I take it that you are accepting
me."

"When my guardian tells you in so many words that he is
agreeable to such a course, the matter will be settled."

Oswald's vanity, despite Miranda's best intentions, had been
pinked. "Hang it, Miranda, it isn't Wingham's face I will see
across the supper table at night." The very thought made him
shudder. "Tell me that you want to be married to me."

Miranda would have given much to say what the usually
affable Oswald wanted to hear. She attempted to speak, but the
sentiment proved intractable. Unable to sit any longer with
even the slightest appearance of calm, she surged to her feet.

Oswald wanted to make it indubitably clear that he had intended no offense in offering for her hand in marriage.

"I am your most humble obedient," he began, more forcefully than humility or obedience could have demanded.

Miranda departed hurriedly from the small sitting room. The vexed suitor shrugged, squared his shoulders, and, without looking at the embarrassed Mrs. Saltfield outside the door, started for the stairs and a consultation with the master of the house.

CHAPTER THIRTEEN

The Devil to Pay

The events of the next twenty minutes deserve to be glossed over. A pained Oswald spoke to Wingham while in Charlotte's presence, managing to look over both their heads. The Earl, staring at a point past Oswald's right ear, offered what he called his heartiest congratulations to the prospective bridegroom. Miranda, called down by an eager Mrs. Saltfield, looked only briefly at a distracted Charlotte while accepting forced congratulations. To Mrs. Saltfield's experienced eyes, this festive occasion resembled none other in her ample memory.

While Mrs. Saltfield chattered with a morose Oswald in the large sitting room, Charlotte gestured Lionel into the hallway. There, between a depiction of a nature scene in Sussex and a statue of a perplexed infant roosting on its mother's lap, she spoke of the next step to be taken in the campaign to convince the London fashionables that Lionel had indeed acted without blame during his guardianship of an attractive young female.

"We must all show ourselves in public as quickly as possible," she said decisively. "You and I, Miranda with Oswald, and your aunt and my parents to ensure unimpeachable respectability. We must all speak and behave as if Miranda's engagement had been planned for many months and indeed that it was anticipated when Miranda came to London."

"Will Badger agree to it?"

"I will ensure that he does."

Lionel chose not to ask himself about the sudden regal imperiousness in Charlotte's tone. A woman confronted with danger to some well-laid plan, he decided, would act like a tigress facing the loss of its young. No further justification was needed.

"There is a supper at the Guildhall, but not everyone you mention has been invited."

"Furthermore, we require an event in which scribblers are likely to appear and even mingle with some of the participants," Charlotte said, and racked her memory for a suitable resolution to the minor difficulty. "Ah, yes, I have it! The Crystal Palace."

Lionel, to be sure, immediately understood. The transparent edifice held an exposition of scientific progress throughout Europe. As its existence had been conceived by Prince Albert, it drew almost unceasing patronage from the Queen. At the eleventh hour of Charlotte's need, she had recollected that Victoria was due to pay one of her visits on this very afternoon.

"Yes, it should do as well as anything else," Lionel agreed. There was a notable lack of enthusiasm in his tone.

Charlotte restrained herself from pointing it out to him. Her reason was perfectly understandable. There was a notable lack of enthusiasm in her tones as well.

Miranda's reading in various periodicals of interest to females had informed her about the Crystal Palace. She knew it had been built in Hyde Park or close to it but wasn't sure which. It was made of glass, or something similar. There were trees on the inside of it, or statues of trees. Beyond the least doubt, however, she was aware that many influential personages attended on special occasions. About the contents of the various displays she knew little and cared less, as was only to be expected from a young lady.

Her mood remained unlightened even by the opportunity to ventilate her best day dress. This was the lovely lilac with sleeves fitted short of the wrists and showing the frilled tulle under sleeves. Such a daring fashion was never likely to be shown in Kent. Nonetheless, her initial fit of the sulks had deepened to a case of the megrims beyond treatment by any patent nostrum whatever. Her features were fine-drawn with tension.

In this particular state of preoccupation, it was no surprise that Miranda had failed to observe the world-famed structure during yesterday morning's ride through some of Hyde Park. Nonetheless she observed that the surroundings were chocka-block with gawkers. Women were dressed as well as possible, powdered and corseted. Charlotte, at her mother's insistence, had climbed into an iron-framed grenadine that made her feel like a spider in a bottle. Lionel, dressed to the nines in a frock coat and gleaming trousers and shoes that looked heavy enough for chopping wood, greeted various dignitaries as if the occasion marked the funeral of a close friend. Miranda took as little comfort in his unhappiness as she did in her own.

Nor did an appearance by the Queen do much to alter Miranda's mood. Victoria, who had been driven to the exposi-tion in an open carriage, was ornamented with her Garter rib-bon and even the Koh-i-Noor diamond on her head. Miranda's father, the late Joseph, had referred to England's Queen as a dull and moral woman who would probably have sold Blighty down the drain if protocol and the royal prerogatives could be observed and her beloved husband, the "Royal ostrich" in Jo-seph Powell's words, could be affected to advantage. With raff-ish familiarity Father had referred to the matronly woman as "Queen Vicky."

While Miranda watched in ever-decreasing enthusiasm and interest, the Queen came into the huge building to a flourish of trumpets. The dapper consort, tired-looking in spite of his ele-gance, held small young Princess Vicky by a hard hand. From the outside it was possible to see the Queen surveying the great crystal fountain as if for the first time. This excrescence faced a large chair that Her Majesty, perhaps wisely, chose not to oc-cupy.

Organ notes were rolling up toward the glass ceiling without causing it to crash as Miranda entered with her party a few minutes later. This was a wonder which she failed to fully ap-preciate also. Only once did it cross her mind, and then in passing, that the slightest pressure might cause glass to break apart, wounding and killing everyone in sight. No greater indi-cation could have been offered to prove that Miranda was in a disturbed state of mind.

"Quite a good notion of the Caliph's," Oswald murmured at her side.

On another occasion Miranda would have chuckled. Charlotte, overhearing from her position at Lionel's side, actually did smile irrepressibly and then stole a roguish look at Oswald. She suddenly shook her head and turned back, putting some added affectionate pressure on dear Lionel's arm.

This aura of good feeling was threatened by her mother, off to the right and glaring up at her husband.

"You see, there is nothing in this hall except for improvements which are currently workable," that lady pointed out to her restless spouse. "No print telegraph, no steel for plating, none of those so-called inventions that can never be of the slightest practicality."

"It is only a matter of time before the inventions you have named will themselves be practical," Mr. Dempster insisted, running a wet palm along the top of his nearly bald skull. "More than one of the scientific tools of the future, in which I have invested, is certain to become marketable—"

"They can be marketed in Covent Garden with the fruits and vegetables, I have no doubt," Mrs. Dempster snapped a little more loudly. "Meanwhile such acute and prophetic vision as you possess has been sufficient to bring your family to the very brink of penury."

Charlotte turned from Lionel and addressed herself to the disputants. "Perhaps it might be more suitable to discuss these matters at another time."

"And another place," Mr. Dempster smiled triumphantly, conceiving that their daughter had come to his aid. "This is not the time or place to go cantering off at the mouth."

"As you are doing *now,* at this very moment," Mrs. Dempster began, outraged anew and properly so.

"Please!" Charlotte realized belatedly that only one known rhetorical flourish was likely to ensure cooperation. "An appearance of amity is needed from both of you."

Those words were possibly stronger than she had intended, but they did reflect her thoughts and proved useful. Mr. Dempster offered an arm. His wife, hesitating long enough to under-score her extreme disapproval of him, accepted it.

Faustine Saltfield had turned excitedly to her nephew, inad-vertently touching his arm with part of the frilled sleeve that adorned her tea-rose day dress.

"He is here," she whispered, containing herself with percep-tible difficulty, her merry blue eyes dancing with excitement. "That journalist is here!"

Charlotte, acute observer that she was, became aware that the older woman was delighted for reasons having little or nothing to do with Lionel's dilemma. There was a girlish plea-sure in Mrs. Saltfield's demeanor, and it caused the younger woman to feel a brief but sharp pang of envy.

Lionel nodded, gratified by this development. "You are al-ready acquainted with the fellow, Aunt. Please ask him to join us."

Mrs. Saltfield sped away delightedly.

Lionel looked at Oswald, seeing enough of Miranda's dress out of the corner of an eye to know that she was in their com-pany. He sensed that Miranda was attempting to meet his eyes with hers, and he regretfully turned away. Charlotte touched him lightly once more, and he brought up a smile from the depths of his being.

The handsome Mr. Roland Travit was turning toward Faus-tine even as she approached.

"I felt certain that you and your titled relation would be among those present on this noteworthy *occasionem cognosce*," he greeted her. "I am pleased to see you again, Mrs. Saltfield."

He made it sound as if her presence was of greater interest than the Queen's. She wanted to ask this personable man if he had seen anyone of questionable repute under the same roof as England's monarch. Mr. Travit was probably blessed with as sharp an eye for hypocrisy as she herself or Joseph Powell on his best day.

"The Earl is also present, yes," she said, mindful of the task that had been set for her. "And his ward as well."

A younger man at Mr. Travit's right hand suddenly looked up. The sharp nose quivered in his thin, long face. Mrs. Saltfield was reminded of some animal as depicted on the wallpaper in Miranda's room, one of those beasts who hadn't yet learned the virtues of thrift and churchgoing and compassion.

"This is Mr. Hebden of *Day's Deeds*, a rival organization," said Mr. Travit, unable to escape the necessity of an introduction. "He is a man who makes one realize that the word 'Mister' is a courtesy title."

Hebden sneered, which Mrs. Saltfield gathered was an acknowledgment of her presence.

She turned to Mr. Travit. "Perhaps you care to speak with the Earl at this time."

"I would be delighted."

He followed her. Not till they were facing Lionel did she realize by looking to her side that the disagreeable Hebden had taken it upon himself to join them.

"This is Mr. Roland Travit," she said after a deep breath, "and someone from a different journal."

Lionel acknowledged the introduction to Mr. Travit of *Society Favors*. He then took the time to elicit Mr. Hebden's name and the nature of his affiliation with *Day's Deeds*. Diplomatically he addressed himself to a point between both men.

"I understand that I have been sought for an interview."

"Your Lordship, it is rumored, not only in the office of *Society Favors*, that you have adopted a ward."

"Correct, yes, Mr. Travit. It pleases me that I am able to put these speculations to rest."

"It is bruited about, further, Your Lordship, that the ward is a female."

"Indeed she is. Triumphantly so, I might add."

Hebden, whose voice was as unpleasant as his appearance, put in, "A female ward who is old enough for various sub rosa purposes."

"That, I suppose, is true."

Hebden looked as if he found it hard to accept his good fortune in being told so much of value by a man who was culpable. As for Roland Travit, however, a deep breath was issuing from between his lips. Watching him closely, Mrs.

Saltfield was convinced the latter had guessed by now that the entire item was deemed of little value by the Earl himself.

"Then I take it you are admitting . . ." Hebden began, pursuing an unattainable objective with a zeal worthy of some reformer in Parliament.

Lionel turned smilingly to one side. "My dear," he called. And, to both men, "This is my ward, Miss Miranda Powell."

Travit was inspecting his colleague's features in order to note changes when the surprise, whatever form it might take, was finally exploded. His own amusement reminded Mrs. Saltfield of Joseph Powell in certain moods. She couldn't remember when some other male had caused her to respond with such warmth. Disparagingly she took it as a sign of encroaching senility on her part. If Mr. Travit wasn't already a husband, then surely a man with his handsome appearance and cosmopolitan vocation would have no need to settle down with one woman. Mrs. Saltfield blushed at the very thought.

Hebden said, "The young lady's appearance amounts to virtual proof that the rumors are correct."

"Not at all." Lionel's urbanity was far from dented by the other's manner. "Standing next to my ward is her affianced, Mr. Badger."

Hebden's face appeared to cave in. Roland Travit glanced over at Mrs. Saltfield in order to share the joke against this colleague he justly disliked. Mrs. Saltfield, pleased by the indication of tastes shared, smiled back.

Hebden recovered his sneer and affixed it in place. "It must have been very sudden, this engagement."

"Not at all," Lionel insisted, speaking for the silent Miranda. "Miss Powell is the orphan daughter of a deceased family friend from Kent, and it seemed only proper to ensure her happiness as best I can."

"That is to say, if I might be pardoned for speaking plainly, that you will provide a dowry in order for her to wed Mr. Badger, whose need for an income is well known to everyone in society and everyone who writes about the fashionables."

"It is to say that I am being of assistance to the daughter of a deceased friend of my family."

There remained another shot in Hebden's locker. "Presumably the engagement won't be taking place until a long interval has passed, giving you time to spend in your home with Miss Powell as company."

Miranda flushed and then turned to see how vigorously Lionel would deal with this most galling impertinence to date. Had she been quizzed in such a manner and were she a man, she would simply have struck out at the tormentor. She looked around swiftly to see if many were nearby to observe Lionel responding so baldly to the other's taunts.

She need not have worried. Lionel's diplomatic smile, reserved at first, did take on a certain edge of contempt. It was enough to cause Hebden to pull back warily.

"The wedding has been planned for October the first of this year," Lionel said, raising his voice only slightly. "Neither Miss Powell nor her affianced will wait any longer to find happiness together."

Miranda felt satisfied, on balance, that he had schooled himself to eschew violence on this occasion but would have been more satisfied with a speech that wasn't so enthusiastic.

Hebden turned away at last, acknowledging that he had been roundly defeated.

Roland Travit laughed. "Once again, Cecil, you have elicited all the facts. The acuity of your probing questions is cause for congratulations yet once more. Those who employ you are indeed fortunate."

Mrs. Saltfield chuckled. Travit grinned at her.

Miranda, looking at Lionel as he greeted a dignitary, heard Oswald whisper, "Couldn't have done it better myself."

She was in no mood to consider Oswald's merits, but it did strike her as presumptuous to compare himself with Lionel.

Oswald suddenly warned, "Smile, Miranda, and look admiringly at *me.*"

Much to the point though the advice was, she couldn't bring herself to follow it. Instead, she was staring down at the floor.

In this stance she suddenly heard a sharp intake of breath from Oswald. "Another challenge has just put in its appearance."

She looked up, but the attempt to focus her eyes precluded her discerning evidence to explain his sudden caution. Nor did she see Charlotte press Lionel's arm again in premonitory anticipation. Only Mrs. Saltfield and she herself remained unaware for moments about the latest development.

There was a stir taking place only a few feet off, and Miranda observed the gay waistcoat and tight trousers and loose tie and ivory-colored shirt belonging to the latest entrant, who was none other than Aubrey Upchurch.

Oswald had already put a hand against her arm, hoping that she would turn around and perhaps not be observed. Miranda was so startled by this latest eruption that she couldn't make the move in time. Oswald deftly stepped in front of her, putting himself between Miranda and the possible future Master of Balliol.

"Ah, it *is* you!" Apparently he had observed Oswald but none other. "I feel certain that if you are among those who attend, as I anticipated, my dear Miranda cannot be far off."

It seemed that Oswald had done a grievous disservice to his own cause by not turning away. It seemed, too, that Aubrey was still managing to avoid the sight of Charlotte and Lionel, not to mention that of Mrs. Saltfield.

Miranda, glancing back of her and wondering if the schoolman's voice had carried to the journalists, noticed that Roland Travit and the detestable Hebden hadn't stirred. Perhaps the immobility was caused by Hebden's wanting to keep an eye on Mr. Travit and the latter's desire to stay closer to Faustine Saltfield. What mattered the most, however, was that both men remained in earshot.

"I am absolutely certain that—ah!"

No doubt he had discovered Lionel's whereabouts. Miranda heard the slurring of footsteps, and then Aubrey was again speaking, though at a pitch that clearly indicated a considerable amount of deference.

"If you recall, Your Lordship, I recently addressed you on the subject of Miss Mir—"

"Yes, I do recall," Lionel said curtly, no doubt wishing he had spoken before any part of Miranda's name could be plain to an auditor.

Mr. Travit, venturing toward Faustine Saltfield to ask whether it might be suitable for him to accompany her on this tour of Queen Victoria's other palace, was halted by the persistent though polite tone that Aubrey was taking.

"Is Miss Miranda present, may I ask?"

Charlotte spoke in Lionel's name this time. "Miss Powell is accompanied by her affianced, who is Mr. Badger."

"What! But that cannot be!"

Another man might have swallowed this bad news with grumbling to himself and nothing more. Aubrey Upchurch, however, was not of this strong and silent breed whose members had done so much to make England the colossus it had become. A pedagogue's training had turned him into the sort who wanted to have everything crystal clear, a man not satisfied to know the climax but who finds himself impelled to repeat the exposition that led to it and insert some descriptive passages as well. A bane to even his slightest acquaintances, he would have been considered a godsend to that storyteller who seeks to introduce an unwitting mischief-maker into the dramatis personae of some harrowing tale.

"But I have not yet formally offered for her!" he insisted. "I am certain that only yesterday Miss Miranda was wholly unaffiliated. I spoke to her at Covent Garden in the morning. She looked so fresh and lovely. It was a sunny day, very warm for the midst of September, I distinctly recall. Now I have to insist upon the opportunity to make my offer, too. Mr. Badger has been most impetuous."

"Quiet!" Lionel had spoken that one word more than half a dozen times, raising his voice a little more with every effort. "You've done damage enough already."

In this perception, he was entirely correct. Hebden was looking from Aubrey to Lionel, and the smile on his lips was even less prepossessing than the usual sneer with which he was identified by all who knew him.

"So the maiden has been under your roof for a while and

unattached," Hebden said. "Truly this will be an item of great interest to readers of *Day's Deeds.*"

Faustine Saltfield was the first to call out her distress, holding back a succeeding cry with one fist over her open mouth. Charlotte, more angry by far, made a move as if to block Hebden from leaving but realized that it was in vain.

Roland Travit took a few steps after the man. Despite her numbness, Mrs. Saltfield noticed the sailorly roll with which he moved.

"You shouldn't do this," Mr. Travit was saying. "The Earl is to be part of an important diplomatic mission for England, and you must reconsider your position as a result."

"If I were even tempted to do so, I know that you would be first in print with the news." Hebden was obviously unwilling to ascribe any patriotic or compassionate impulse to a colleague.

"I give you my most solemn word," Mr. Travit began, but the other had left. Mr. Travit shook his head in silent apology to Faustine Saltfield for not having been of aid.

No one else moved, each accomplice knowing full well that the fat was now in the fire.

CHAPTER FOURTEEN

Bad News Is Received
and Transmitted

The balance of the day proved as difficult as might have been expected. Lionel sat gloomily through the Lord Mayor's supper at the Guildhall. Charlotte, at his right, felt no better. Collectively they presented an imposing portrait of unhappiness.

Nor would Miranda's presence at this juncture have been of use in offering good cheer. She was immuring herself in her room, where she remembered Lionel's deep voice and striking eyes along with the moments of ecstasy during which they had been close together and had kissed.

Oswald sensibly foreswore the company of his distracted affianced, choosing to spend his time at Boodle's. He was unable to play at cards, however, because he was short of the necessary and couldn't raise a loan. He watched the others, his own misery mounting at the sight of such execrable play and the appalling victories that followed.

Faustine Saltfield, like Miranda, was thinking about a gentleman toward whom she experienced strong feelings. No doubt Mr. Roland Travit, having tried so hard to be of help, would want to see her again. He might decide, however, that he couldn't possibly be welcomed in Jermyn Street. That prospect saddened Mrs. Saltfield almost beyond belief, considering how briefly she had known the journalist.

No record exists of Mr. Travit's emotions or activities for the balance of this day. It may reasonably be inferred that he didn't pass the time in a halo of unalloyed happiness.

By morning, for such is the power of a night's rest, Charlotte and Oswald and Lionel and Miranda had separately made the same profoundly moving discovery. They had concluded that the damage being done was preferable to waiting for some blow to fall at any unexpected time. Responses could be made to known accusations and matters resolved conclusively one way or the other.

Lionel's rash of optimism was encouraged by the sight of a beaming Mrs. Saltfield entering his study next morning. In one hand she carried a copy of *Society Favors*.

"Mr. Travit was as noble as his word, and our difficulty isn't mentioned."

"An excellent augury," he conceded.

As one result he was ill prepared for a perusal of the freshest copy of *Day's Deeds*. The threepenny paper, which grandiloquently called itself "An Illustrated Journal of Romantic Events at Home and Abroad," had been purchased by Grimm at his master's order. The butler eased it on a tray over the Sussex wood desk in Lionel's study as if he didn't want it suspected that he had ever touched this publication.

"Umf," said Lionel.

The news item was written in a sniggering tone of which he didn't doubt that Hebden was a master. At the end there occurred a plaintive question in Latin: *"Quis custodiet ipsos custodes?"* Who, indeed, would guard the guardians?

"Oh, dear," said Mrs. Saltfield after even a perfunctory look at the distortions in Lionel's features.

"The matter will be a two-day wonder and nothing more," he said quietly. It didn't occur to this practical man to ask himself what excesses might take place during those two days. It was a consideration that Miranda would not have overlooked.

A series of knocks sounded deferentially against the door. At his call it opened on Grimm.

"A visitor, Your Lordship."

He was expecting Charlotte. "Ask Miss Dempster to join us here."

"I beg your pardon, sir, but it is Mr. Upchurch who wishes to speak with you."

Lionel was in no mood for any communion with the cause of his downfall, as he had categorized Aubrey after yesterday's revelations. Nevertheless, a brief discussion might give reassurance that outsiders were responding to the occurrence in a supportive manner.

"Ask Mr. Upchurch to join me in the large sitting room," he said.

It was here, at a midpoint between the gleaming mantel register at one side and a whatnot of bric-a-brac from many nations on the other, that Mr. Aubrey Upchurch could shortly be discerned. He smiled politely, waiting to discover what attitude the Earl would be taking in light of those recent infamous developments.

As the Earl showed no indication of essaying speech, the guest took it upon himself to do so.

"Your Lordship, I am anxious to make it clear that my love for Miranda is firm and unwavering," he said with the vigor of a first-rate batsman striding onto the cricket field. "I yearn for the day, the moment, when I may hold Miranda in my arms and crush her to me."

Mrs. Saltfield, who had entered behind her nephew, was beginning to feel surfeited with declarations involving passion and promises of passion. It was not difficult to believe that the lady was somewhat wiser as well as older.

"Begging your pardon, sir—and madam, to be sure. I cannot accept it that an engagement, and especially one to a gentleman of no means such as Mr. Badger, is irrevocable."

Once delivered of these sentiments, Mr. Upchurch was content to occupy the next minutes in deep breathing, at which he demonstrated himself to be enviably proficient.

"By the same token, the swift onrush of events, the taint of suspicion, though no more than a taint, I feel sure, impels me to remind myself that my own fate vocationally is connected to a certain standard of (shall we say) irreproachable behavior. For that reason, and with the greatest reluctance, I must pass up my claim on Miss Miranda until (if I might express myself this way) the sky clears again."

"Yes, I certainly understand." Irritable though the other's sanctimonious manner made him feel, Lionel was convinced that if nothing worse happened as a result of Aubrey's revelations, the matter would have been satisfactorily resolved on all sides.

"Please assure Miss Miranda that my heart beats with hers."

Mrs. Saltfield put in, "I shall accept that commission in time and give her a truthful account 'of the extent of your unselfish feelings."

Aubrey's eyes narrowed on her, alerted by that choice of words. Ingrained courtesy would not let him give voice to the suspicion that had crossed his mind.

"And now, perhaps," Lionel said instantly, "you will be good-mannered enough to leave Mrs. Saltfield and myself to our own devices."

Grimm entered shortly on the heels of another series of warning knocks. This time the smile on his lips was more genuine, as he wasn't carrying some odious threepenny journal on the proffered tray.

"There has been a messenger with correspondence, Your Lordship."

One look at the seal on the missive and Lionel asked himself why it had been possible to muster his optimism of the last minutes.

"How serious is it?" Mrs. Saltfield asked. She had taken a chair after relocating six gewgaws intended for display on the round table otherwise infested with miniatures of apple-cheeked young girls.

"It is from the Earl of Aberdeen." Lionel's voice was almost sepulchral. "He asks to see me before day's end."

"There may be some new matters that confront the Elgin Commission."

"Of course there may be, Aunt, but I would venture ducats to an old shoe that if so, they don't concern me any longer."

"Perhaps the Earl wishes to show his confidence in you by

putting you on another task alongside the current one. That also is possible."

"Show confidence? My dear aunt, Aberdeen is a politician. Part of his calling requires the prompt jettisoning of everyone who might offer the least problem. If you go on a ship with someone of that eminence, his primary task is to get rid of all the lifeboats but one and have that one guarded so he can board alone in case of difficulty."

"You are feeling too unsettled, dear," Mrs. Saltfield said pacifically. With that pronunciamento issued, she sat back to wonder how soon it would be possible for her to encounter Mr. Travit again.

In the next half hour, Lionel indited a note in which he promised to visit Aberdeen at Downing Street before day's end. He wanted to discuss his feelings with some special person and promptly asked his Aunt Saltfield if Miranda was likely to be awake by this time.

"I cannot be sure unless I was hiding beneath her bed," the latter retorted with some asperity.

A ring of the bell on the table closest to his chair was enough, as ever, to summon Grimm to the large sitting room.

"Ask Miss Miranda to join me here."

Recognizing that she would soon be politely asked to leave, Mrs. Saltfield rose. As which juncture, the door opened on Charlotte Dempster, who had once more rushed in without waiting until her presence could be announced.

No greater evidence of her present condition could be found than in the lack of detail she had taken with her rig-out. A tuft of blond hair had been permitted to straggle away from the tortoiseshell comb hard by her neck. Not only were creases defacing the dark full skirt, but she was wearing both a short jacket and a velvet cloak over it. Only some prodigious upset would have caused the normally equable Miss Dempster to show herself publicly in such comparative disarray.

"You have seen the threepenny nonsense, of course," she was saying with such velocity that an alarmed Mrs. Saltfield had to shut the door in case any passing servant should overhear. "Have you realized what must be done about it?"

"Truth compels me to say that I have been exercised by a communication from Aberdeen. He has requested an interview before this day's end."

With a wave of one gloved hand, Miss Dempster brushed away any consideration of matters involving the future course of the British Empire.

"There is only one hope," she said.

"Yes, and in time we will indeed live down any condemnation, little deserved though it has been. The passing years and the contentment of our marriage are going to enable me to return once again to the arena of diplomatic endeavor."

"Something decisive must be done before the Queen and her consort are announced to their Maker."

"What do you have in mind?"

"In order to still the gossipists as soon as may be, the date of Miranda's marriage must be put forward."

"But surely October the first is soon enough!"

"To you and me, yes. To the gossipists, probably not."

Lionel found himself deeply disturbed by this new plan, more so than by any previous catastrophe. The reasons for such strong feelings were difficult for him to comprehend, but his protest was immediate.

"Any attempt along those lines will be thought of as an indirect admission of guilt."

"People who don't know us are certain to feel that some outrage was perpetrated. By following my new plan we provide additional time for the sensation to cease and be replaced by another."

"Will Oswald Badger agree to accelerate the time for his nuptials with Miranda?"

With main force Charlotte kept from snapping that Oswald would probably have accepted a ceremony taking place at the Regents Park Zoo with each participant dressed as a monkey. The income that would follow his marriage to Miranda was the justification for it. As she, too, was forced to marry for money, Charlotte was aware of considerable bitterness in her thoughts.

"I can arrange matters with Oswald," she said firmly.

Lionel nodded. Only a fool would have been unable to appreciate the wisdom behind Charlotte's strategy.

"We were almost unable to discover a suitable church for the original date," he pointed out a little weakly, well aware that no other sensible objection remained. "It will be utterly impossible if the time is put forward again."

"Then the marriage must be performed here, in this house, and invitations sent out accordingly."

"And the new date you suggest?"

"One week earlier than previously intended." Charlotte's wide, wide smile was proof that she felt herself under considerable tension. "September twenty-fourth."

"This Saturday?"

"On that date, Lionel dear, Miranda must become Mrs. Oswald Badger."

"Agreed," he murmured after a moment, with a glance at the ceiling to ask himself how Miranda would behave when this latest bulletin was transmitted.

That question answered itself immediately. The outer door had suddenly opened. It did seem, Lionel couldn't help feeling, that anybody could come into a room of the establishment as if he was a publican.

Miranda, overhearing the news, raised two shaking hands to her flame-red hair and emitted a gasp that could have been heard as far off as her native Ryehurst in Kent. Then she let out a cry and turned and ran off.

Lionel, deeply stirred by an outburst from so lovely a child, started after her.

"*I* will soothe her," said Mrs. Faustine Saltfield, moving to the door like a stately galleon and thereby giving the girl time enough to begin exhausting herself in tears. "She must be angry at you."

Lionel halted. He realized grimly that it would be wisest for him to see as little as possible of Miranda until her wedding to Oswald Badger. It was the best action he could take for his own benefit and for Miranda's as well. No reflection was likely to have been more maddening.

Slowly he turned away. Calling upon his deepest reserves of diplomacy, he mustered a smile to display for Charlotte.

CHAPTER FIFTEEN

A Chapter of Accidents

It can be stated with confidence that the day did pass.

Before that happy event, Lionel determined to his satisfaction that Miranda was no longer in tears, having obtained a statement to that effect from his aunt. Feeling a little better, he sailed forth to Downing Street and his dreaded discussion with the PM. He knew that he was going to be relieved of his duties with the Elgin Commission because of the scandal about his private life.

Miranda was unwilling to be moved from her chamber. Mrs. Saltfield eventually desisted from persuasion, but only after getting a firm promise that Miranda would be more biddable on the next day.

Charlotte went off to a fitting for her own wedding gown and managed her time so adroitly as to encounter Oswald Badger near one of his usual haunts. They spoke politely, but added substantially to the communication by use of their eyes. Oswald did manage to touch Charlotte's right hand in bidding her a fond farewell. Charlotte rubbed the glove across her cheeks a number of times after leaving him.

The evening had its pleasures for Mrs. Saltfield at first. She had sensed a taste for music-hall entertainment in Mr. Roland Travit and felt that he might well be among the attendees at a newly opened establishment of that nature in the Blue Anchor Lane, not far from the seafarers' domiciliary area called Stepney. She herself, as has been previously noted, was a fancier of the type of entertainment that was likely to be offered.

The building looked up-to-date on the inside. Hundreds of rich, red upholstered seats gleamed under various glass lighting fixtures.

Of Mr. Travit there was no sign until the first interval. He greeted her warmly, then offered his regrets about the recent happening at the Crystal Palace. Mrs. Saltfield briskly absolved him of blame. It was understood between them that he would call upon her when Miranda's nuptials had been concluded.

Toward the interval's close, the elegant Mr. Travit was reminiscing about the start of his career. He had been employed by another newspaper at that time. Assigned to the task of reporting a sermon at the Spanish and Portuguese synagogue in Bevis Marks hard by Aldgate, he had been horror-struck when the Hebrew clergyman spoke in a foreign language and didn't feel better until a succinct translation of the remarks had been eventually offered.

She was still chuckling at the image of a befuddled young man as the interval concluded. It seemed right and proper that he should take the empty seat at her right, but she hesitated to let him hold her hand.

It was just as well she did so, as she found herself enthusiastically applauding the tumult of acrobats and dancers, dramatic sketches, recitations, and dioramas moving noisily along on rollers but showing scenes of unparalleled splendor.

Just before the *tableau vivant* that was to conclude this performance, a singer came out, a blond young woman with fine eyes that could be seen through a glass borrowed from Mr. Travit. Her figure was outlined by spangled clothes that hinted without revealing. Little wonder that she was greeted by a thunder of applause.

Her singing was pleasant enough, as it turned out, but different words had been applied to currently popular melodies, and the words dealt with events in the news. There was a lyric about Queen Victoria and her family, which was just this side of indelicate. Another dealt in not-too-warm terms with relations between the British and the French, and a third commented wryly about Mr. Benjamin Disraeli's penchant for ultrafashionable raiment. A fourth song lyric approved the Crimean "problem" and took strong issue with the Czar of Russia. There was a burst of applause and then she began another ditty, once more with words grafted onto a currently popular tune. She sang in a plaintive little-girl voice:

> Who will keep guard on my guardian,
> Although he's a peer,
> Let me tell you, my dear,
> He plays as only a male
> hale and hardy can.

Mrs. Saltfield was horrified, and not at all because of the appropriation of a Latin aphorism. She sat transfixed and completely unaware that Mr. Travit had reached out a hand to offer comfort.

The second stanza dealt with the nameless but recognizable peer "wandering" into a certain bedroom other than his own. Mrs. Saltfield could endure no more of this unfounded mockery. She surged to her feet and started for the nearest aisle so that she could make her exit from this infernal den, not caring that several voices protested her action.

Mr. Travit stayed in place, knowing that he could do or say nothing helpful.

The next day, a Wednesday, passed with more mentions of a wicked peer in those threepenny journals, including that of Mr. Roland Travit's employer. Faustine Saltfield was absolutely certain that Mr. Travit hadn't indited that particular infamy or that if he had done so it was under duress.

On that same afternoon Mr. Stanley Briggs, a Member of Parliament from the Ilfracombe area and a component of Her Majesty's loyal Opposition, rose in the commons, took off the hat worn by seated members, and asked a question. It concerned the behavior of a certain peer who was not, as it happened, named. It concerned, too, the unfortunate prevalence of loopholes, as he called them, in adoption procedures throughout the realm.

A considered response was made, rebutting each of the Honorable Member's doubts in full. Attention was distracted, however, by knowledge of the cabinet rank of that officer who responded. Some wit articulated the general feeling by letting it be known that the choice of the Home Secretary for that particular task had been hideously inappropriate.

It became known that a comment upon the matter was made on that same day by Queen Victoria herself.

The monarch happened to be the recipient of a visit by the family physician, Sir James Clark. Having ascertained that the health of her youngest, Prince Leopold, left little to be desired, Sir James reported accordingly to Her Majesty.

"Youth is always a time in which great care has to be taken," said the thirty-four-year-old Queen sententiously.

"To be sure, ma'am."

Victoria could easily think of unpleasant consequences in which treatment such as she received might not be available. In giving birth to Prince Leopold this past April, she had consented to permit the Scottish anesthetist, Dr. John Snow, to relieve her pain with chloroform. Her acceptance of the innovation and its success would be of great help in lessening childbirth's pains for all women. Because of that willingness she would be many times blessed, and for the most cogent reasons.

"It is unfortunate about the Earl's obsession with that child." The Queen thereupon made the comment which she would preserve in one of her many journals and repeat in an informal letter to her niece, Princess Adelaide of Hohenlohe. "There is a most regrettable lower-class air to the entire situation."

And on this day the Earl of Wingham, "temporarily" relieved from duties in the world of diplomacy, announced further details of his ward's wedding. Rather than taking place at St. George's, Hanover Square, or St. Peter's, Eaton Square, the vows would be taken at the Earl's home in Jermyn Street. The date of this solemn occasion had been advanced one week to September twenty-fourth, the coming Saturday.

CHAPTER SIXTEEN

Woman's Wiles

Miranda had not accepted the inevitable, feeling that every step she took was actually in preparation for her marriage to Lionel. In better times her imagination adroitly paraded disasters as logical developments. Now that she faced a dilemma without any favorable resolution in sight, her beleaguered faculties communicated the conception that a happy solution would materialize for her and Lionel.

Not till Friday morning was it possible to bring Miranda out to Cleveland Row and Mrs. Bell's shop. Here she was to fit the bridal gown that had quickly been run up for her. The founder of the establishment specialized in such costume as riding habits, family mourning dresses, and rig-outs for balls. Corsets and bridal gowns were added specialties of the celebrated Mrs. Bell, which Miranda discovered belatedly. She had been on the point of seeing herself married to Lionel—for she intended marriage to no other—while wearing *une grande tenue* suitable for riding an elephant.

Before starting out, Mrs. Saltfield, who was to accompany her, had asked Charlotte to join the gathering. Miss Dempster, generally so obliging and courteous, had rejected the opportunity with few words.

Miranda, like Miss Dempster, was in a querulous mood. In her case, it took the form of searching out complaints and enunciating them.

"My hair isn't done," she said, looking at it in the triptych mirror.

"That will be seen to, Miranda, before the ceremony," said

Mrs. Saltfield with more patience than that dame had thought she possessed. "It will have to be arranged in bandeau, half puffed at the sides and crossed in front by a plait taken from the back hair. Flowers will be arranged so—and so." The dressmaker, Señora Cuellar, kindly illustrated the pattern by using her gentle hands against Miranda's bright red hair. Miranda realized she was also being difficult with this woman who had never done her the least harm, and smiled in appreciation.

"The top," said Mrs. Saltfield, directing Miranda's attention to the gown which was, after all, the primary item on their agenda, "is quite lovely."

At any other time Miranda would have enthusiastically agreed.

"It would do nicely for a ball," she said, making an exception only because the Spanish dressmaker was in earshot. "For the particular wedding that is supposed to take place shortly, it leaves everything to be desired."

Mrs. Saltfield counseled herself to be patient. Cunningly she employed a variation of the Socratic method of argument.

"Do you dislike antique moiré?"

"Not that, no."

"Have you any objection to the top being low upon the shoulder?"

"I don't."

"Are you vexed because the garment is *demi-basque* in front and behind?"

"No," Miranda whispered.

"Do you cavil, then, because it is covered almost entirely with white blond lace?"

Miranda shook her head, not trusting herself to make a denunciation of that breath-catching example of the dressmaker's art.

"It cannot be that you are averse to the three rows of blond that will ornament the corsage and that now drape the sleeve."

Another headshake. This time it was almost imperceptible, made that way by Miranda's feelings of shame and her inability to lie.

"I consider the point settled," Faustine Saltfield said drily.

Given so sharp a challenge, Miranda returned to the fray. "I don't care for the lower half."

In this statement, too, she was tampering with the truth. The section thus named was covered by three blond flounces overlapping each other. Two more were painstakingly looped up at the side by clusters of flowers with branching sprays.

Mrs. Saltfield's response this time shrewdly manifested itself in an incredulous silence. Her basic point had already been made.

"I must have new slippers," Miranda insisted, covering her flanks now that she was in full retreat.

"You will certainly have them."

It was impossible not to feel sympathy for the girl. As Faustine Saltfield's mind ranged across the breadth of the difficulty, she discovered what seemed a perfect contention to move Miranda at long last.

"You have told me that you respect and admire my nephew," she said briskly. "It seems to me that you can show it best by cooperating in full, by realizing the motives for his position in this matter and accepting them forthwith."

She would not have anticipated the nature and quality of the response thus obtained. As Señora Cuellar busied herself with various eleventh-hour changes of no real importance, Miranda suddenly gave a wide smile. It wasn't that she had seen the hot white light of pure reason. Palpably she was a young woman decided upon the only possible course of action to be taken.

"Yes," she said cheerfully, "that is very true."

Mrs. Saltfield, experienced in dealing with females of various ages, abruptly stopped hoping for a simple resolution of the matter.

"I must indeed cooperate," Miranda was saying now. "I have to be a good and willing girl, a proper ward who is not only loyal and obedient but also grateful. Above all, I must be grateful."

Mrs. Saltfield would have been the last to dispute that point, but something about the eagerness with which it was put was enough to make her regret her part in the entire discussion.

"I must show you this," said Miranda, smiling as she opened the door to her guardian's study.

She found a pensive Lionel sitting at his imperial desk of Sussex wood. It was late in the afternoon. Pen and ink were in front of him, a container for sand to dry his writing at the left, but papers weren't in sight. Any material that could concern diplomatic endeavors was no longer part of his life, nor was it going to be until that certain matter in his private affairs had been resolved in a way that the cheap press and the Earl of Aberdeen considered favorable.

He looked up, startled that Miranda had entered without knocking. The radiant and lovely face was in view, the achingly beautiful fresh features, the wide forest-green eyes, the fair skin and fiery red hair and lovely chin with only the slightest, rakish little jut to it, in his opinion, and nothing more. Indeed, that, too, was entirely to his taste as was every element of her features.

"I wanted you to see it first," Miranda added, gesturing down at herself, "considering all that you've done to help me."

At which point Lionel realized that his ward was wearing what had to be the dress in which she would shortly be married to another. The added beauty was so astonishing that he called out even as he recollected his manners and stood quickly.

"You mustn't show this to another man before the ceremony," he insisted, speaking as if all the words were one. "It's very bad luck."

"Only if the groom sees it beforehand is it considered unlucky." Her light laugh seemed to ripple over the study. "And you aren't intended to be the groom."

He looked at the radiant young woman, and some shading in her eyes caused him to say a little sadly, "I couldn't possibly be the groom."

"All the same," Miranda said, determined that no remark he made was going to wipe the smile off her face, "I do want to know what you think of it."

She turned around, permitting him to see her figure from the back. During the pause, she allowed herself to feel thankful that Faustine Saltfield wouldn't interrupt, as she had left the house to join Charlotte on an expedition that involved Miranda's scheduled marriage. Miranda in her turn, as might be expected, took not the slightest interest in what she was determined wouldn't occur.

The smile was back in place as she turned to a dazed Lionel once more.

The Earl of Wingham had to swallow air before he was able to speak again. "You're—*it's*, lovely. Very lovely indeed."

"You almost said, 'You're lovely.'" Miranda was drawing closer and was already halfway around the desk on the way toward him. Whispering, she asked, "Did you mean that, Lionel? Truly?"

The Earl of Wingham was no fool, nor could it be said that he was unfamiliar with the wiles of the fair sex. He knew quite well that Miranda was making every effort to enchant him. Part of his mind was amused, but a greater part of it was awestruck because of the success she was having. He felt immobile, eyes wide, palms raised, lips dry. He could feel ten toes curled up somewhere in the depths of his shoes.

"I have never denied for a moment that you are attractive." Speech from him was required now, but he experienced difficulty with the words. He couldn't make them out even as he spoke, and possibly Miranda couldn't, either.

"I wonder if you just think of me as comely," she said, halting her progress toward him, "or you like the person I am."

"Oh, I like you very much, very much." A member of the lower classes, conversing in so agitated a tone, might have been said to be babbling. A peer, however, would be slanged as no more than distracted. "I feel much affection for you, Miranda. Much affection indeed."

"In that case, I must acknowledge your sentiments and show my own very real affection for *you.*" Once more she was moving closer, which tested Lionel's self-control to the uttermost. "I must show the gratitude that you expect from a loyal and devoted ward."

So saying, she put her arms around him and puckered her lips.

Lionel made an instinctive attempt to turn a cheek toward

her, so that it alone would be the recipient of her gesture, but his own feelings proved too much for him and their lips met. It suddenly became impossible to sever the connection. Moments passed deliciously.

His heart was hammering when the demands of continued existence made it necessary to let her go and catch his breath. They were at the point of smiling toward each other. Certainly Miranda had entrapped him on purpose, but no man could have been more willing to fall into a trap. For the first time since very young manhood, the Earl of Wingham was in love.

As for Miranda, she well knew that her choice of garment with its special association had helped make the point to Lionel at last. He knew he loved her, and with the same strength as she loved him. There was a basis of shared understanding. Each knew the other's mind in vital areas but could still be intrigued and delighted by the other's strength and will. Miranda felt certain that the vagaries of fortune had caused her to discover the only foundation for a happy marriage.

It was impossible not to feel regret about the future of that rare female, Charlotte Dempster. Nevertheless, Miranda couldn't overstate the importance of Lionel's being as happy as possible. Miranda didn't doubt that happiness with Charlotte would have been of a different and far less impassioned quality which he no longer wanted.

Thoughts of Charlotte were occupying part of Lionel's dazed mind as well. It was absolutely necessary to apprise her of this development. As for Oswald Badger, the Earl didn't doubt any longer that in spite of his continuing need for money the young man was respectable and even worthy. The knowledge of his true feelings about Miranda had helped him view other people with greater charity. Oswald didn't, however, care for Miranda in a husband's way. Happiness with Oswald would have been of a different and far less impassioned quality which she no longer wanted.

Neither was prepared for a sudden deferential series of knocks on the door. Miranda had moved away by the time

Lionel called out weakly. The door opened on Grimm, that most affable of butlers.

"Miss Dempster has arrived and wishes to see you, sir," said Grimm.

CHAPTER SEVENTEEN

Lionel Is Bearded in His Den

Charlotte had interrupted her affianced when in Miranda's company several times in the past. Indeed, such unexpected appearances were rapidly becoming a tradition of the house, as Lionel wryly found himself thinking. Never before, as it happened, had she been so weary in manifesting herself at such a time, or so determined.

A fresh consideration had been occupying her mind through the late morning and into the afternoon. Rather than take Lionel's time to discuss the matter immediately, though, she had temperately followed the day's schedule and permitted Mrs. Saltfield to join her on a quest for accommodations to suit Miranda and that young man to whom she had been summarily affianced. Miranda herself had not been available for this quest, or claimed not to be. A bride's traditional nervousness was apparently dictating her responses.

The matter of accommodations was eventually settled. Faustine Saltfield rushed upstairs for a lie-down before supper. It now became possible to give time and thought to her most pressing concern.

Lionel, still startled by Charlotte's entrance, belatedly remembered the mission with which she had entrusted herself. "I hope you and my aunt were able to find a suite for Mr. Badger and—"

"Yes." Instead of waiting for the conclusion of that sentence, she turned to Miranda. "I have made arrangements for you and —and Oswald, of course—at the Clarendon Hotel on Hans Place, where the food is excellent. You can occupy rooms there until a more fitting domicile is found over a longer period of time. I feel certain that you will approve."

"Thank you." Miranda's smile was warmed by a rush of sympathy at Charlotte's having lost the finest man in the world. "I am sure it would be suitable."

"It *will* be suitable," Miss Dempster contradicted firmly. Only then, looking more closely at Miranda to drive the point home, did she realize that the younger female had come into her own affianced's study to display the bridal gown. "Most attractive, but I am not certain it is suitable for a showing here and so soon."

With the rebuke lightly administered, Charlotte turned. "Something of importance has occurred to me, Lionel dear."

"And to me, in a sense." Lionel smiled tentatively.

"I will insist, if only this once, upon the prerogative of a lady."

Not only had Miranda declined to leave in embarrassment after having been criticized however mildly, but she chose to interrupt the conversation.

"In fact," she said lightly to Charlotte, "you have come to beard the Lionel in his den."

"I will ignore that," Charlotte said with pseudo-austerity, but there was an appreciative glint in her eyes almost in spite of herself. She wished that her affianced hadn't chosen to share his own appreciation with the perpetrator first.

"I know that the date of our wedding is December the seventeenth," she said, calling the meeting to order, "but I have come to the conclusion that we should bring it forward."

Lionel was perhaps too stunned by his good fortune for further speech at the moment. Indeed he resembled nothing so much as a fish gasping out of the water.

Charlotte had decided against offering any explanation for her attitude. It couldn't be of the slightest use to tell him that upon emerging from the Hotel Ibbetson at eleven ack emma she had encountered Oswald Badger. He pretended to have been strolling in the area, but she sensed immediately that he had been waiting to see her.

Brief as the conversation had been, partly for the reason that they were on Oxford Street, Oswald had nevertheless made his presence felt. With his marriage to another being only a day off, he could no longer deny his true feelings. For the first time he declared that he loved her and none other, that he could never love another. He wanted Charlotte to rush off with him to Gretna Green and a quick marriage. Never could he have been so persuasive and sincere, having obviously given the matter much thought.

Charlotte had heard herself responding frankly. With the greatest clarity she informed him that she'd have ventured with him to Gretna Green or France or even the former colonies in America. She was not, however, alone. Her elders had to be considered now, being on their uppers because her father had improvidently put money into inventions that were unlikely to earn him as much as a bent farthing. If she didn't do what was necessary at this time, her parents would shortly find themselves on the street.

Only reluctantly had Oswald Badger accepted this restatement of truth of which he was already aware. A broken man, he had walked away slowly.

Charlotte's decision to accelerate the time to her wedding with Lionel had followed as a matter of course. Determinedly, as has already been remarked, she faced him.

He started to say, "But I must make it clear—"

"My feeling is that October the eighth will be satisfactory," Charlotte went on a little more loudly. "If St. George's is not available for the date we now desire, Lionel dear, we can take a leaf out of the book of Miranda and her—and her affianced. We can arrange for the ceremony to be performed in this house."

Lionel found himself impaled on the horns of a dilemma more acute than he could have originally expected. Realizing that Charlotte, the childhood friend he had promised to marry, was already upset for some reason, he couldn't help being reluctant to add a further shock to her system. The reminder that Charlotte's parents would be facing a life of poverty came to him almost like a blow. He was aware that he might offer to put Mr. Dempster on a retainer for some trumped-up reason. The searchers for scandal would alight upon such an arrangement, too, however, and evolve discreditable reasons for it. His return to a career of service in the Diplomatic could be aborted as a consequence almost before the PM began considering it.

Lionel was attempting to frame a response that would be tactful but at the same time wholly uncompromising. Such faculties for negotiation as he possessed, although honed to a sharp point by the needs of governmental maneuvering, were strained past his capacities.

"I am so glad that we have settled the matter, Lionel dear," Charlotte said, logically accepting his silence as a sign of approval.

Miranda gasped, but would expend no outrage while in Charlotte Dempster's presence.

"I can only hope that I haven't been high-handed, but surely you can understand a bride's impatience." Charlotte's smile was courtesy itself. "Now what was it that you wanted to tell *me?*"

"Nothing." Lionel presented a picture of misery that would have wrung the heart of anyone who was in love with him. "Nothing at all."

"As we have agreed so completely, Lionel dear, for which I am truly grateful, it is fitting that I return home to let my parents know immediately about the change in our plans."

She was turning to go but recollected her duty to her affianced. Hurrying back to Lionel, she raised herself and kissed him on a cheek.

"You are a dear, Lionel dear," she said with such sincerity that no one could have questioned her genuine feeling of friendliness.

Having smiled agreeably at Miranda, whose glowering features she was too frayed to inspect or even notice, Charlotte finally turned to go. Gently, as might have been expected, she closed the door back of her.

Lionel waited until his affianced's steps could no longer be heard.

"I will inform her of the true situation between us, Miranda. You have my solemn promise."

At the sound of his voice addressing her, Miranda choked back a cry and lifted her bridal gown before running out the seldom used back door of the study and up the stairs toward her room. Lionel could hear that she was making every attempt to subdue the volume of her wrenching sobs.

Over the next few minutes it would be impossible to talk with her. Lionel wanted to let Miranda know that his newly evolved plan called for a full and frank exchange of views with Charlotte and her parents over at the Ibbetson. No other solution presented itself.

Deciding that Miranda would be amenable to reason after the lapse of time that had now taken place, he walked out by the front door of his study and up to the second floor and along the hallway. Here, as if to guard against him, he encountered Mrs. Saltfield pacing at the side of an edgy Pam.

"The poor child is dreadfully upset," said that Cerberus who could speak. "It is the night before her wedding and she favors seclusion."

Lionel took it for granted that his aunt knew nothing of the root cause behind Miranda's unhappiness. That particular mistake put him more at ease with her.

"Please ask Miranda to speak with me."

"At the moment she must be in tears and would not want to be viewed by any male whatever. Including Pam." She patted the top of the bulldog's head.

"How short a time will it take, do you feel, before the spring is dried?"

Mrs. Saltfield shrugged decorously, as became a gentlewoman.

"In that case, please inform Miranda that I have set out to hold a discussion with Charlotte and her parents. Upon my return, you may add, I will be able to assure Miranda that the difficulty between her and myself has been resolved."

Mrs. Saltfield looked startled, then pleased. Lionel became aware for the first time that his aunt knew of his and Miranda's feelings toward each other.

"I shall do so as soon as may be," Mrs. Saltfield promised. "Good luck, Lionel."

It crossed his mind to offer some celebrated aphorism along

the line that luck is the province of those who are prepared. In this particular circumstance, however, he chose to forgo an appearance of dauntless heroism. It was enough that he embarked on the mission.

CHAPTER EIGHTEEN

In Which It Is Shown That Catastrophes Are Ill Timed

He had rushed into the street, determined to ease the tenseness within him by walking to the chosen destination. Streets were comfortable enough for late September, and he soon found himself considering their picturesque denizens. A water-cart man's raised voice sounded almost exactly like that of his whinnying horse. The persistent music of a barrel-organ man allied with his wife's frenetic tambourine movements almost deafened Lionel. A sandwich-board man called profanely as the well-dressed peer hurried by.

From a minor functionary at the front desk of the Ibbetson, Lionel soon discovered that Miss Dempster and her parents had left the sanctuary. There was no way of being sure when they might return. He grimaced at the thought that there wasn't a negotiator in Britain, no matter how well prepared in accordance with the aphorism he had nearly quoted to his aunt, who could have expected a setback of this type.

He decided to pass the time by walking around this vicinity. One step followed another in such fierce energy that he soon found himself in a less respectable area he couldn't immediately identify. In attempting to return by foot, as no cab was available that didn't look as if it had been trampled, he found himself at Bankside, which he recognized in part because of the river and its unmistakably muddy water catching glints of the fading sun. He was a long way from his native habitat.

His senses were suddenly assailed by a group of street musicians. A harpist, a violinist, a bored-looking trumpeter, and an emaciated woman at the bass fiddle stood in a line and played dolefully. In front of them, and facing the sparse group of passersby, was a middle-aged woman in an ecru chip-poke bonnet and a cloak that had assuredly seen better days. She was speaking loudly, almost as if at him.

". . . Demon rum," she orated. ". . . Fight liquor and rally against . . . save yourselves from the curse of drink, which destroys home and fireside . . ."

Lionel moved a little more quickly. He would have to pass almost in front of the lectern before he might escape to even the scruffiest cab and return to the purlieus of Oxford Street and the Hotel Ibbetson.

The speaker suddenly drew a deep breath. Lionel sensed that his posture and clothes were being briefly but searchingly considered.

"There," she said, and Lionel felt certain that she was pointing at him, "is a fine example of a rich bloke who must be a drunkard. Would he find himself near the docks in all his finery, otherwise? No, he's recovering from a session with the bottle, a living proof of the wickedness of strong drink."

Because he was moving more quickly, Lionel cannoned into an opened box of leaflets at his feet. The squibs sailed along a twisting path to join many that had previously been crumpled and tossed away. Lionel's deeply bred instinct was simply to halt long enough to apologize for the damage and then help pick up the squibs.

"Can't even walk straight," the speaker said sarcastically, and Lionel knew he had remained in place too long for his own best interests. "Look at this, all of you, and see what will become of you if you aren't careful."

Half a dozen of the witlings, impelled by curiosity to observe this horrible example in such splendid finery, presented themselves in his path. He was unable to stride toward freedom, as he thought of the long street ahead of him.

Someone growled, "Oughter be shamed 'a yoursel', so you ought!"

It needed another moment for Lionel to understand that the members of this crowd, standing in place, meant him no harm and couldn't offer the slightest impediment to his leaving.

The speaker, anxious to drive her point home with even greater emphasis, asked him, "Aren't you well and truly sorry for what you've done?"

Lionel's training in relations with persons from foreign climes caused him to feel that it would be wiser to make his departure on a cordial note.

"Not sorry at all," he said, so loudly and clearly that every auditor must have known he hadn't been imbibing after all. "But I will say, ma'am, that you have given me an excellent idea of how I should spend the night."

A chorus of jovial and sympathetic laughter followed. Several men cleared a path for him, and he was allowed to make his escape at last.

He might as well have stayed for all that his return to Oxford Street accomplished. The Dempsters had not yet returned, making it impossible to speak frankly with all of them about his desire to wed another.

As it was past six o'clock by this time, he decided that a drink would help to invigorate him. Truly the temperance speaker had made an impression upon one listener at the very least.

The nearest bastion for refreshment was located, inappropriately enough, on Charlotte Street. Here, in a tavern named the Goat and Grapes, he was soon gratefully facing a portion of Scots whisky. Scruffy-looking bohemians in smelly clothes stood around the dim-lit room and talked in loud voices. Others played darts. No one was turning in his direction. This area's residents consisted of unsuccessful artists and flat-voiced singers with an occasional penny-a-liner thrown in. By no means were those the same sort of people he had unwittingly encountered at Bankside.

A soft-voiced man was sitting next to Lionel. Upon finishing his third drink, the man started talking to him.

"Service was an 'ard life for me," he singsonged. " 'Elp at mealtime, be the coachman when the master and missus or the children want ter go aht, make repairs on the coaches and even risk me life fighting a fire when one 'appened to break out. All this for five shillin's a week and found. Let me say I was glad to get out of it at long last and despite a sacrifice in earnings to try me 'and as a sculpture."

The image that was conveyed had no discernible effect upon restoring Lionel's equilibrium. He turned away so as not to be observed chuckling, and at that moment his eyes lit upon a curious sight.

No less a personage than Oswald Badger, a day before his scheduled wedding to Miranda, had come into the establishment and disposed himself at a scantly lighted table in the far end of the room. There was a grim expression on his handsome features, and the usual ready smile was wholly absent as if it had never been. Lionel wondered almost idly if Mr. Badger often visited this tavern on Charlotte Street near the hotel where Miss Charlotte Dempster lived with her parents.

More to the point at this juncture in his affairs, Lionel saw no way to leave without running the risk of observation from Oswald Badger. Courageously he approached the bridegroom-to-be and looked down at him until their eyes met.

"I will never escape," Oswald Badger said mournfully, strong drink having put a slur on the ends of his words. "As time proceeds and I embark upon such projects as eating or sleeping or even dreaming, one of Miranda Powell's connections will appear before me and claim that I am not disporting myself in a fit manner."

Lionel was on the point of saying that an arrangement for such an escape was part of the task upon which he had set himself. He preferred, however, to face as few questions as possible from this source.

"Will you do me a favor?" he asked carefully.

"Your Lordship, I am in the process of doing one for you and will have completed it by this time tomorrow." He squinted thoughtfully. "Not that Miranda isn't a fine girl, indeed she is. It is only that—ah, well, there are private sorrows which every man faces."

Lionel was not in the mood to hear a consideration of Miranda's nature from anyone who might visualize even the slightest defect in it.

"Would you be so kind as to accompany me to the Hotel Ibbetson?"

"To—pardon me?"

"I am planning to have a discussion with Miss Charlotte Dempster and her parents. It seems to me that perhaps your presence would be useful."

It had occurred to Lionel while speaking that if Mr. Badger did indeed have strong feelings for Charlotte, she would be comforted in knowing that she was able to attract males other than Wingham. True, no female in her senses would care to link her future with a young man who didn't have any prospects at all of obtaining the needful, but Oswald was likely to be of use if he waited below while the conversation proceeded and went up to the rooms for a visit with Charlotte a very short time afterwards.

"Why, yes, I would be happy to see darling Char— Miss Dempster, again." Having confirmed Lionel's intuitive conviction about his true feelings, Mr. Badger rose swiftly. He was aware of Lionel watching him sway against the table and then in the opposite direction. "If I may pardon you for a moment—I mean that if *I*, your most humble obedient, may be pardoned."

"Certainly."

Walking with the greatest care, Oswald proceeded toward the darkest portion of this *estaminet*, where not a table or much of anything else was to be seen from here. Evidently he knew the geography of the Goat and Grapes quite well.

Lionel had been waiting for only a few minutes when his attention was distracted, and he turned around. A somber-looking gentleman with one foot against the bar rail was facing most of the patrons and calling for their attention.

"Please to direct your eyes in this direction," said the somber man loudly, if not with excessive grace. "Before my assistant passes among you to receive a token of your esteem, it is my intention to put on an exhibition of skill that is sure to earn your admiration as well as any coppers you can spare."

Lionel found himself a little taken aback to see that the officials in this place would permit such an intrusion, but realized that it was likely to rate as additional entertainment. The patrons seemed willing to give their attention at least.

Rather than exhibiting some form of skill known to Lionel by hearsay, the mountebank behaved like a lunatic. As Lionel watched, the man displayed a thin taper and lighted the far end of it from a candle at the closest table. Turning the implement around, he then drew the fiery end toward his open mouth.

Somebody in the audience called out admiringly. Another man encouraged this fool's action by a burst of applause.

Lionel was aware that it could be indiscreet to antagonize the patrons by interfering. Nonetheless, it behooved a far-seeing man to be prepared for a calamity. In a purposeful manner he approached the bar. From the wet surface he picked up a half-filled beer glass and positioned it along with himself so that he could douse the looney at the first untoward sign of difficulty.

The madman put the fiery end between his lips, inserting it deeply into his mouth.

Lionel was far from prepared for the next happening, and so was everybody else. No one had seen Oswald Badger leaving the stygian darkness, nor could anyone have known what his views would be about the sight meeting his eyes at this point.

Oswald had not heard that the deed was being done in hopes of raising money for the performer. That particular intelligence might have caused him to feel a strong sympathy. He would even have taken the man aside to ask if the hours of work were at all onerous. As it was, however, he knew only that a man seemed determined to put an end to his life by committing felo-de-se in public. It had forcibly been borne upon him during the last minutes that no one should ever give up hope, the Earl having been about to make it easier for him to see Charlotte again at a time when Oswald had despaired of doing so before his nuptials to another. Looking around him almost incredulously, he saw that no one was moving to halt that suicidal fool, that some few witnesses seemed admiring. Of the Earl himself, a lightning-quick glance around gave no sign.

He acted swiftly, reaching for the torch and removing it from the man's mouth. No doubt his gesture caused the man some pain, as the latter doubled up with both hands over that orifice. He was keening furiously at the same time.

His colleague took justifiable umbrage.

"Why, yer—" he raised both fists.

But it was the fire-eater himself, still keening, who took action. He straightened himself and, in a prime example of what Oswald would ever regard as human ingratitude, raised one fist only and used it for thumping Oswald on the chin.

Another man plunged into the fray, but this one didn't take Oswald's side. It seemed as if almost everyone in the room was feeling the same lack of sympathy toward the man who had attempted to save the life of another.

Lionel, outraged, plunged into the burgeoning melee.

The barmaid, buxom like all of her tribe, had reacted placidly to developments until this point. Now, when she saw the day's profits evaporating and faced the possibility that the Goat and Grapes might turn into a charnel house, she called out to all participants to put a halt to the fray. It was too late, however, for this gesture of compassion.

Lionel struck once and then a second time. Before he could land a third punch he was aware of two men behind him, each gripping an arm. Immobilized, Lionel told himself urgently that there wasn't any more time for him to indulge with others in this sort of bestial high spirits.

At that moment, a third groundling planted himself in front of the peer and struck him to the right of the chin. Lionel closed his eyes unwillingly, his head fell back, and he knew no more.

CHAPTER NINETEEN

Faustine Pays a Visit

Faustine Saltfield was inspecting herself disapprovingly in the
full-length mirror in her room. She was not at all satisfied with
the girth that identified her reflection. A long full skirt in black
would hide some of it, however, for her appearance as a matron
of honor at the wedding next day.

The bride's guardian, to whom she wanted to show what she
would be wearing, was still away from home. That was decidedly unusual. Could it be that the attempt to resolve his feelings
toward two different females had caused him to commit some
damage to himself?

Mrs. Saltfield felt far too experienced in the ways of the un-
gentle sex to rush after any member of the species. Nevertheless, she took no relish in uncertainty at a time like this.

If only to allay her own worries she made a point of querying
others discreetly. The smiling Grimm didn't know where his
lordship might be found. Neither, as it happened, did that
queen of housekeepers, the dour Mrs. Jossy. It crossed Faustine
Saltfield's mind idly that those two might make a spectacular
married couple, but she was in no mood to pursue the speculation.

Miranda was looking out the window of her room when Mrs.
Saltfield interrogated her. The young woman seemed expec-
tant. Interestingly enough, she conveyed not the least impression of having any midriff at all. Mrs. Saltfield decided that if she
herself could be seated more often it would be helpful in returning to her that sylphlike figure she had borne in youth.

"No, his lordship hasn't returned, but I expect him momentarily," Miranda said. Alarm shaded her leafy-green eyes. "Could anything be wrong?"

"No, dear, of course not."

Mrs. Saltfield didn't know if her assurances had effectively cloaked her own concern. She knew that Lionel had let Miranda be aware of his schedule for the day. The child was imagining that no difficulty existed. Various courses of action were occurring to Mrs. Saltfield as she returned to her own room.

Pursuing the matter with Miss Dempster might well be awkward. Faustine Saltfield declined to request any of the servants to make inquiries at hospitals and would never have considered entering into discussions herself with a member of the uniformed police force.

She wished there was some male with whom she could pursue this matter. As usual, in thinking well of the opposite sex these days one man's name and image leaped first to her mind. This, to be sure, was none other than Mr. Roland Travit.

She was well aware of the difficulties with which she was strewing her path, but to every objection she could conceive a suitable response. Mr. Travit was certainly discreet. Overhearing a confidence, as he had shown in the recent past, he wasn't the man to betray it. Furthermore, if he decided that inquiries ought to be made of various officials, he would do so, and perhaps while in her company. With his own position as a journalist, he might obtain intelligence that would not be vouchsafed to a woman.

Even if Lionel perversely took it into his head to make an immediate return home, she would at least have spent more time with Roland Travit, this man of whom she was so fond and who appeared to reciprocate. The prospect recommended itself highly indeed.

Before setting out upon this expedition, she changed into a dark dress with a horsehair underskirt that would minimize any slight imperfections in her figure.

So excited had she been by the vista before her that only when she confronted a hansom cab driver did she realize that she was entirely unaware of Mr. Travit's home address. She was not, however, unused to navigating about London after dark, thanks in large part to her fondness for raffish entertainment in the music halls. She made up her mind, as a result, to obtain the necessary information at the office of that journal which employed Roland, as she was now thinking of the redoubtable Mr. Travit. Never before had she entered a place of business, but on this occasion she felt she could offer a good reason for doing so.

"Can you take me to the offices of the newspaper called *Society Favors?*"

"Just you 'op in, missus, and I'll get you there in the outside of no time."

The Irish driver could not possibly have been as good as his word, but the efforts he made were certainly creditable. Mrs. Saltfield wasn't aware how little time passed before she found herself near Highgate and was actually let off in front of a gray two-story building near the center of Hornsey Lane.

Without further delay, she entered. After passing a hallway she found herself in a strange but not unoccupied room. Two elders in smocks could be seen in the far corner, manipulating a machine which she correctly assumed was a printing press. A sour-looking gent with square-rimmed spectacles and an eyeshade sat behind a scarred wooden desk. Seeing that the visitor was well dressed, this one rose, smiling, and introduced himself as Mr. North, owner of this far-from-gigantic enterprise.

"And here is a copy of *Society Favors,*" he offered grandly, hoping to see a smile of gratitude on the visitor's frozen features.

Cluttered print on the unfolded sheet described social and sporting events, with advertisements in the four corners and moral sermons occupying what would otherwise have been blank spaces. Daubs of ink were transferred to the tips of her fingers as she made the courteous effort to look, however briefly, at the material that had been thrust upon her.

"We're a four-pager to avoid the tax stamp," Mr. North said gleefully in a squeaky voice that suited his appearance. Mrs. Saltfield understood that he considered the small size of his broadsheet to represent an achievement because Her Majesty's Government was consequently being deprived of revenue.

"I would like," she said, speaking carefully when it occurred to her that he might otherwise not understand a gentlewoman's English, "to find Mr. Roland Travit."

"He's not *h*ere," said Mr. North, taking such care with his aspirates as to confirm that he probably wasn't standing too far from his place of birth near the sound of Bow Bells.

"I would like to have his address at home."

"Afraid I can't be of assistance, ma'am. It's a rule not to give out the addresses of any of our workers."

She started to point out that as the owner he was in an excellent position to disregard any rule without suffering ill consequences. Antagonizing this man even mildly would be unsound, however, nor had she accumulated any experience that involved the use of bribery.

Mr. North realized in turn that she didn't have the least intention of moving.

"If you must stand there, ma'am, I—well, I certainly won't give you his address, but as it's somebody like yourself who wishes to see him, I can say that he'll be here shortly. He's been sent out on a special job tonight."

A wait that endured for what seemed an endless time now took place. Mrs. Saltfield occupied a wooden chair which disposed her weight so gracelessly that she decided to stand instead. The smocked elders applied themselves to producing noise, and she dreaded to think what else.

The place also made her uncomfortable because it was unpleasant to look at. Droplets of ink had formed jagged patterns during the years and befouled the wooden floor. Windows were streaked. Specks of dust rose at any slight breeze to perform a harlequinade of carelessness, a dance of dirt. Mrs. Saltfield's instincts toward cleanliness, honed by the presence of staff in every home she had ever occupied, made her respond to these signs of usage by turning away to look elsewhere. Eventually her eyes fastened on the door through which she herself had come.

Two males entered as she was watching. Each was offered a surly nod by the owner and then walked out by the door at the farthest end.

Mr. Travit himself was the third to come in, his sailor's walk fully in evidence. He had outdone himself sartorially with a high-cut waistcoat that revealed little of the shirt underneath. His trousers were surprisingly loose, and he carried a felt bowler in one hand.

At sight of Mrs. Saltfield, his brows rose. Before she could speak, he said briskly, "In a while I expect to be able to give you my time."

And he walked to the other door, as the first two had done.

She had been pleased to see him even briefly, but Mrs. Saltfield was a prey to mixed feelings now. Surely it would have been far more sensible not to have come, and she was strongly tempted not to risk being made to feel like a fluttery old beldame. Nonetheless, Roland would be emerging from that door within moments. She found herself putting off a decision and wasn't entirely surprised that her mind remained to be made up before Mr. Travit returned.

"Let me take you to the visitors' room," he said, and walked in front of her out the nearest door and along a bare hallway. He managed to be first into a small chamber with perhaps a dozen wooden chairs and one scrofulous desk of the same material. She had dreaded seeing others present, but the place was empty except for them.

"The Earl has gone without telling any of the staff about his destination or when he would return," she said, presenting the difficulty to him at last. "That is extremely unusual."

"And tomorrow is his ward's wedding day." The journalist looked thoughtful. "Has he found the prospect of marrying her off to be particularly upsetting?"

"My nephew has been upset by so much else that I cannot give a coherent answer."

"Obviously, his whereabouts have to be learned before the event. And obviously, too, I must keep any newsworthy discovery to myself or I shall lose your regard, which I am frank to admit I value most highly."

For the second time he was turning his back on the possibility of vocational advancement in order to assist her and her relative. She had been titillated on the first occasion by her capacity to influence him, but now she was moved.

Mr. Travit's possible sacrifice had plainly moved him as well. There was a look on his face unlike any she had seen for years in a male.

"This may not be the best place for it," he suddenly said, with a glance at the closed door, "but for a regrettably brief interlude it will do."

She felt herself being soundly kissed, and happily returned the pressure. This contact could have been even further removed from the perfunctory despite their both being past the age, as she considered it, for such sportiveness. Mr. Travit, showing a streak of caution that she reluctantly approved, drew back.

It was difficult to pull her thoughts together. "But what is to be done?" she asked. Her voice, in addressing Roland, was far from the fluting tones which had issued from her so often in the recent years. "About my nephew, I mean."

"First we will go back to Jermyn Street," Mr. Travit responded with hard-won decisiveness. "It is necessary to find out whether or not he has returned."

"And if not?"

Mr. Travit considered. Any number of possibilities suggested themselves, but Wingham was unlikely to appreciate another's actions in starting up a hue and cry as a result of what was almost certainly a harmless delay on his part.

"Then we will wait," he said firmly.

Mrs. Saltfield began to protest, but decided upon accepting the advantages of entrusting this difficulty to the hands of someone as worldly as dear Roland.

"Of course," she agreed in the mildest tones of which she was capable, "we will wait."

CHAPTER TWENTY

Miranda Pays a Visit

To Miranda, cursed by her lively imagination, it was clear why Lionel remained absent. He had failed to communicate with Miss Dempster and couldn't bring himself to return and say so.

At ten o'clock she made certain that he had not yet materialized. A decision formed itself immediately in her mind. Returning to her room, she put on a simple dark cloth cloak and gray bonnet, almost hiding her dark green muslin from casual sight. Her next step was to borrow the money for a cab.

For this purpose, she interviewed Mr. Grimm. The butler smiled and was regretful, or so he said, but inflexibly declined to advance coppers. Falsely he claimed that he had no coins whatever nor access to any. Mr. Shakespeare's sentiment about a man who could smile eternally and remain a villain came unbidden to Miranda's perfervid thoughts.

Mrs. Jossy, the dour housekeeper, was more forthcoming. A florin, two shillings, a sixpence, and a threepenny bit were offered and accepted with gratitude. Even as she promised to repay, Miranda suspected that the coins wouldn't be sufficient for a cab.

For once, her dread suspicion proved to be accurate. The cabbie sneered at her proffered payment for a ride as far off as the Hotel Ibbetson, a name which Miranda recollected Charlotte giving as her temporary domicile. The driver agreed to let her off near that destination, however, in exchange for the small hoard. Her meager coins paid for a ride as far as Hardcastle Street, north of her destination.

People walked unceasingly back and forth as Miranda hur-

ried. A young woman with dreadfully poor clothes was hugging
a three-color talma mantle around her neck, touching the or-
nate needlework and massive fringe of the garment that didn't
suit her at all. A pair of heavily painted girls were conversing,
but their eyes swiveled right and left all the while. One woman
nursed a baby as she was in motion. An older man in a toff's
dapper rig-out was scratching himself as he walked. Dozens of
children were on the street at this late hour, which was more
shocking to Miranda than anything else she saw.

She passed the Ibbetson without identifying it and had to
return. In order to reach the front desk it was necessary almost
to joust against a number of clergymen and other males she now
considered as callow youths.

The suite number and floor upon which the Dempster contin-
gent could be found was eventually revealed to her. Miranda
hurried upstairs, apologizing to members of the clergy as she
moved.

A small woman with gray hair opened the correct door.
Miranda's first guess that it was a maid who confronted her was
soon altered. This woman looked too much like an older version
of Charlotte, though without the latter's intelligence or serene
disposition.

"My daughter has just returned with us from a day and night's
activities," said Mrs. Dempster querulously at Miranda's initial
request for a visit with Charlotte. "She faces yet another wearying day and cannot therefore see anyone."

"Won't you tell her that Miss Miranda Powell must speak with
her at this time?"

"Have I not just—oh. Oh! You are that ward of Lionel's, and
who has caused him so much notoriety. Well, wait here and I'll
see what my daughter wishes to do."

The door was closed on her, though not shut. Miranda realized that Charlotte's mother, like herself, had been dressed in a
wholly different fashion and seen in another light entirely at the
recent joint expedition to the Crystal Palace. It was therefore
unsurprising that neither had recognized the other upon re-
newing an already tenuous acquaintance.

The door soon opened, but only part of the way.

"Please come in," Miss Dempster's voice invited her.

Upon entering, Miranda was able to see why the young lady hadn't shown herself. She was wearing a white merino nightgown cut a little low and a fringed half cloak of pitch-dark material over it.

"I am sorry if your reception to date has left something to be desired," Charlotte said with that delightful smile to which Miranda had become accustomed over the recent days. "Permit me to take your cloak, and I will join you shortly in the sitting room. At your left."

This chamber, which Miranda entered in moments, left much to be desired. There was an out-of-style monopodium table and crocodile couch. The Tavistock chairs belonged to a different era. There was a Gypsy teapot with its belligerent-looking spout and the wooden bars upon which it rested. A coal scuttle gave unneeded warmth, perhaps conforming to the residents' concept of luxury. It was impossible not to feel dismayed by the total lack of such amenities as photographs or reproduced paintings or even a small piece of sculpture. No better evidence could have been offered that it was not a home in which the possession of money was taken for granted.

"You see me here in my native habitat," Charlotte said a little ruefully as she entered in turn. "A poor thing, but my own. Mine and my parents."

Miranda looked down. "I would wish to say that everything is most attractive and without an unseemly opulence. The words are nearly impossible to come by, and a suitable tone as well."

It wasn't a statement she would have made to an ordinary female under any circumstances. Miss Dempster, however, was different. A liking that clearly existed between these two was enough to make deception wearying and even shameful.

Having inspected this area, Miranda could understand more easily why Charlotte had become so determined to improve herself. Miss Dempster had been planning to do Lionel a great service in partial payment for the financial security that was being offered with his name. She would be a staunch friend, a superlative hostess, a compassionate mother, the sort of woman whose airs and graces would make the Earl a man envied by his elders and equals alike, an asset to any diplomatist at home or away. It was unfortunate, from such a point of view, that the Earl had inopportunely fallen in love with another.

Nonetheless Miranda was aware of the urgency of discussing the difficulty which had brought her to this place.

"Did Lionel wait upon you here during the day?"

"If he did, I wasn't here to be seen. My mamma may have indicated to you that we were all attending to various familial duties of a social nature."

Probably that was a reference to some visits made to wealthier friends of long past, those who had offered loans to the impoverished elders.

Miranda could now hear Miss Dempster's progenitors involved with a discussion in which tones, as words could not be distinguished through thick walls, were almost musical. A fortissimo passage would be followed by a scherzo con brio, and a recitativo staccato was only a preface to an arietta with some distinctive tremolo passages.

Miss Dempster was disregarding the fracas, having schooled herself to do so over a long period of passing time. Miranda, attempting to duplicate the feat, fell prey to occasional winces. Charlotte thanked her silently for not making any comment about that unwelcome intrusion.

A cadenza with a bass counterpoint was beginning when Charlotte asked, "And why would Lionel have wanted to see me during this day when I had already come back from Jermyn Street?"

There was no other course than for Miranda to make the point directly, her suspicions having been confirmed. If she regretted Lionel's inability to have done what was necessary, she had to show by example that more responsible behavior could be followed.

"He wants to wed me and not you," Miranda said quietly.

Miss Dempster's upbringing had schooled her to accept adversity in any form. Rather than protest, she bit her lower lip and looked away.

The silence between these friends, difficult enough at any time, was growing unbearable.

Miranda added, to reinforce the point, "And I sincerely want to marry him."

It was impossible for her to decipher the play of emotions that crossed Charlotte's upturned features. Miranda couldn't have known that Charlotte Dempster had first felt that any woman who didn't want to make her life with Mr. Badger was the most unlucky of creatures. It then came to her that Oswald was going to be freed of an alliance just as she would. They might find themselves bereft of the needful, and her parents might suffer even more than they were doing presently, but circumstances could change in some as yet unknown way. For the first time she felt stirrings of hope within her.

Seeing Miranda's regret at having brought the news, Charlotte almost smiled.

"It must have been very difficult for you to say those words to me."

Unable to speak any further, Miranda nodded instead.

"My dear friend," Charlotte said, and drew out her arms to accept the other.

Each was well aware that a difficult time lay ahead, but it was beyond both their powers to consider such matters in detail at this moment.

The friends embraced, both of them close to tears of happiness for each other and themselves.

CHAPTER TWENTY-ONE

An Idea
Is Conceived and Lost

Two wheels of the cart suddenly bumped over a stone. The fresh impact of wheels against cobbles was enough to raise the Earl of Wingham to a groggy wakefulness. His eyes focused with difficulty on early morning light and then on the conveyance which was carrying him. It happened to be a two-horse cart with flaking paint.

"I'm being taken to the guillotine," he murmured aloud. "The rabble have twigged the actual worth of aristos as a class and we're all of us off to Madame la Guillotine."

It was an arcane first thought for a man waking from enforced oblivion. Spoken aloud, it startled his companion. Oswald Badger, whose bewildered eyes had been open a little longer, said what was expected of him.

"Have you any idea where we are?"

The cart wheels were making a slightly more metallic sound. Lionel looked out. They were riding over Blackfriars Bridge and not far from Ludgate Hill. It seemed unlikely that a guillotine had been set up so close to St. Paul's.

A somberly dressed man with a black stovepipe hat was sitting in the driver's perch.

"You there!" Lionel called. "Where are you taking us? Stop this cart right now."

The man turned, showing ugly features. "Takin' you away from the Goat and Grapes is where, as I'm bein' paid to do. Farther, the better."

"If you'll drop us off," Oswald Badger said, joining the conversation now that he seemed able to concentrate, "you'll save time for everybody."

"Well, now! If you two gents want to go anyplace where my 'osses and self can take you, it's only right and proper for you to say the word and it'll be done. Allus supposin' you 'as some brass to back up the request, mind!"

Coins had fallen out of Lionel's pockets during the fight which a not-quite-sober Oswald had caused from humanitarian reasons, but several shillings remained.

Lionel said to his companion, "It's better if he takes us to, say, Piccadilly, and we get a cab there."

Oswald agreed. Two well-dressed men on foot in this general neighborhood, St. Paul's or no St. Paul's, were likely to be set upon.

While the jehu was turning his vehicle around, Lionel had time to examine his colleague in dishevelment. Oswald had been pummeled at least as severely, but seemed to have taken the matter and its resolution in stride. Anyone observing these two was likely to think that it was Oswald who had come to the rescue of a besieged peer.

Only with the greatest difficulty could Lionel bring himself to consider what was likely to happen when he got back to Jermyn Street. Charlotte would have arrived early, prepared to witness the wedding of Miranda to another. The news of that change in plans which he and Miranda had made would be warily communicated just before the intended ceremony.

Charlotte would retreat, feeling terribly wounded. He was likely to be unsettled himself at having caused distress to somebody of whom he had always been fond. As for Miranda, she felt a keen liking for Charlotte, which he had happily observed despite his recent worries, and was likely to be made miserable by the effects of that necessary communication. There probably wouldn't be a smiling face to be observed along the length and breadth of Jermyn Street, it seemed to him.

"Will you come back with me?" Lionel asked.

Oswald looked down at his clothes, which were the best in such wardrobe as he had been able to afford. A stop back at his room would be useless from the point of improving his appearance.

"I can make some final touches before the ceremony," he said, agreeing to accompany Lionel.

Not until that moment did the Earl recollect that it was Oswald who had been scheduled to commit himself in marriage with Miranda. A few well-chosen words at this juncture would settle the one aspect of the matter and settle Oswald's place in the day's activities. Mr. Badger's hopes of a future of affluence would apparently be dashed. Lionel refrained from giving the bad news so soon after what he and Badger had been through. It was no time to destroy the man's hopes. Besides, he did want Badger joining him at the house, where he might offer some consolation to Charlotte. It was the same wish that had helped create the difficulty last night, but the consequences this time couldn't be disastrous.

Silence had descended between the passengers, causing the driver to glance around.

"Not been an 'alf-bad time," he said, perhaps to keep them from engaging in physical unpleasantness and doing some damage to the vehicle that hadn't yet been done. "Went to five buildings, me an' 'enry did, an' we told the landladies that somebody in each was moving. Then we 'urries in an' takes all the belongings an' loads 'em on this cart and brings 'em to a—a friend 'oo buys for pretty good prices. Ah, but won't them people be shocked a caution when they return 'ome an' see as everythin's been carted off?"

Oswald Badger was distracted, nodding. Beyond the least doubt he was used to conversations with members of all levels in society, having encountered them during such adventures as the one he had recently shared with a reluctant Lionel.

"It just shows," Oswald said, with a tact that Lionel found as impressive as it was unexpected, "that London isn't safe, as it used to be."

Lionel was on the point of snapping that it was the act of theft to which the other was referring so casually. Badger's approach, however, was likely to gain more in the nature of that goodwill which was needed now.

"I thinks of me and 'enry as moving men, cully," said the bus driver, showing a philosophical side to his nature. "But what I will say is that it's a sin an' a shame when you see the cheap an' stinkin' clothes an' furniture as most people live with. Makes me feel like I'm doin' a favor by takin' that rubbish away from 'em."

There was a distraction when two passing hay wains caused traffic to halt. The driver made that sort of whickering sound which Lionel associated with horses rather than drivers, and the cart was once more under way.

Lionel didn't want any silence just then. "It won't be long."

"I know," said Badger.

"You're not looking as contented as a bridegroom ought to."

"I have never seen a contented man who was due to be married," Oswald remarked. "They are on tenterhooks. They make terrible jokes. They look from right to left like hunted stags. Worse yet, if a bridegroom-to-be encounters an attractive female new to his acquaintance, he flinches as if he had just broken several commandments at the same time and thinks about his choice of a wife over and over again."

Lionel flinched as if he had just broken several commandments at the same time. It went unnoticed.

"As a group," said Oswald Badger, concluding his soliloquy on an optimistic note, "and until the ceremony has been performed, they seem among the least happy of mortals."

"And you, Badger, are suitably unhappy."

"Partly because I recently found myself in a physical affray where I received a hiding. Some signs of discomfort are bound to result. You may remember the occasion."

"I have cause to remember," Lionel said, with another wince. "Nonetheless, you look as if you would appreciate knowing that the ceremony had been called off."

It had occurred to him that the speculation offered at this time might cause Badger to feel some consolation when he finally discovered that Miranda was not going to marry him after all. It was a matter of giving the preliminary indications so that the letdown would be easier. No doubt there was a term for that process in the highest reaches of diplomacy, some French-derived word that Aberdeen used in frivolous conversation with a cosmopolitan personage like, say, Mr. Disraeli.

Normally, Oswald Badger would have radiated good cheer and insisted that nothing could be further from his mind than serious reservations about the prospects that faced him. He might have concluded, as he often did in polite discourse, by referring to himself as the listener's "most humble obedient." On this particular occasion, disturbed by the memory of jarring fisticuffs and the physical closeness of different classes in the social fabric, Mr. Badger was infected by an attack of honest speech.

"There seems no reason why I should not be enthused," he admitted, more glumly than called for. "I am to be married to a girl I may not have long known, but of whom I am most fond. I might add that it is certainly possible for a man living closely to Miranda Powell to become even more fond of her with passing time. I concede all that."

Lionel felt that Mr. Badger was only displaying the good taste that was to be expected of a soundly brought-up young man. It was inconceivable that anybody could know Miranda over some period of time and not sooner or later be madly in love with her.

"Do I take it, then," he asked patiently, "that you have no wish to be married at this time? Possibly there is a wild oat or two that you have not yet sowed."

"Oh no, no," Mr. Badger protested, putting a palm up to his jaw. "I have experienced quite enough of intemperateness and have known little adventures with women as well. That is not the difficulty."

"I await, with decreasing patience, I fear, a further explanation."

"It's quite simple, really. You see, Your Lordship, I do want to be married at this time. Truly I do. But Miranda—well, she wouldn't be my first choice as a bride."

Badger's discomfort caused Lionel to guess what was being hinted.

"Charlotte, then? You want to marry Charlotte Dempster?"

"Yes," said Oswald Badger, looking down as if he expected

that he would be accursed forever by his companion. "I love Charlotte."

"Hm, I see," Lionel said.

As if he was uncertain of having convinced Lionel of his ardor up to this time, Badger looked up wistfully.

"She means everything to me, Charlotte does. She is light and shade, sunshine and night, trees in the arboreal dell—"

Lionel had the feeling that if he heard anything more about arboreal dells he would gnash his teeth.

"Yes, I do see, my dear Badger. I understand perfectly. Charlotte is a fine female, truly a splendid female. I applaud your judgment."

"But you don't seem angry!" Oswald Badger was startled. "If someone else wanted to marry the woman I love, then I would chastise him or give serious thought to doing so."

Lionel disregarded that. "I have a difficult question to ask you, one which requires an honest answer. In light of my having tried to help you during the recent perils at the Goat and Grapes, I hope that you will oblige me with the honest answer I crave."

"Certainly I will make great efforts to do so."

"It is not the effort that is required, but the honesty," Lionel pointed out severely.

"Very well then, Your Lordship, you shall have it."

"In which case, I consider that I have received your word as a gentleman." Lionel paused, framing the exact words he wanted to use. "Do you have any reason to believe that Charlotte returns your love?"

A look of anguish passed over Oswald's face. Perhaps he wished he had been submitted to the tender mercies of the guillotine itself rather than forced to give the true answer. But he had made it clear he would do nothing else.

"I believe she does, yes," he said quietly. "She has never said anything to that effect, but she has looked at me in ways that make her true feelings clear. There is something tender about her at those times. The gray eyes develop little tawny flecks when she sees me, as they always do when she's happy."

Lionel had never observed the phenomenon, but it said

something for Badger's sincerity if he had done so and considered it deeply.

"Your frankness, Badger, deserves a similar response," Lionel said, deeply moved. "Fond of Charlotte though I am, Charlotte would not be *my* first choice as a bride."

"Do you mean that there is another woman in your life?"

"It is Miranda Powell whom I wish to marry."

Oswald didn't speak again until he had thoroughly digested this intelligence.

"Then Charlotte and I—there is still hope for me with her?"

"Apparently, but this news is not likely to do much for your finances."

"Something else may happen. Unlikely though it seems, perhaps one of Mr. Dempster's myriad investments will turn out favorably and she will be able to marry the one she chooses."

"That is all very well, Badger, and I appreciate your feelings. But you are overlooking a problem which deserves to be addressed with the greatest keenness of intellect that either of us can muster at this time."

"Problem? Something else?"

"Precisely. Miranda knows the extent of my feelings for her, but Charlotte must be informed of the new developments as quickly as may be."

"I can only suggest, as I cannot possibly do it myself, Your Lordship, that you tell Charlotte the truth in a frank and above-board manner."

"Tell her, you mean, that she and her parents will rot in poverty because of my seeming fickleness. I can assure you and her that never have I been so stirred as by my darling Miranda and I know that never will I be so moved again. But the consolation to the Dempsters for such assurances would be meager indeed."

Oswald chose not to point out that the same condition applied to him. "If only I hadn't been so selfish and had learned to work at something! It needn't have been important, and could have taken only an hour or two of my time every day. I could have been a surgeon or a banker, some such minor craft to occupy only a little time."

An idea was hovering at the edge of Lionel's brain, but he felt too dazed to reach out toward it. He knew very well that it would be of the greatest importance if only he could bring himself to accomplish that one feat.

" 'Eere we are," the cart driver called out.

They were at Piccadilly, and in the throes of leaving the cart in a gingerly fashion, paying the driver a shilling for his service, and discovering a cab to return him to Jermyn Street with his guest, Lionel let the idea flee his mind. He knew very well that it was a decidedly unfortunate turn of events.

CHAPTER TWENTY-TWO

Journeys End
in Lovers' Meetings

At Jermyn Street, he found wedding guests entering. The quickest of greetings were exchanged at first, Lionel being aware that he wasn't dressed to the limit of his capacities and wanting, for that reason if none other, to cut short the preliminaries. At his side, Oswald Badger was speaking cheerily to friends and acquaintances, behaving as though he was in perfect fettle and everything was due to proceed as scheduled.

"Upstairs," Oswald said breathlessly to Lionel during the shortest of pauses. "Charlotte is in the small sitting room. Your housekeeper just told me."

Lionel hadn't seen the dour Mrs. Jossy at all, but nodded. "I'll join Charlotte in moments. You might want to prepare the ground, so to speak."

"Indeed, yes."

Lionel was inching his way toward the staircase, defending himself against colleagues and friends among what seemed like shoals of well-wishers. Hardly had he reached the first step than he was aware of a sight so uncommon that it demanded at least a moment's attention.

His Aunt Saltfield was seated on a sand-colored stuffed settee. Rather than exchanging politenesses with guests, she was looking deeply into the eyes of a dapper graying gent. Further, she was holding hands with him.

At this astonishing manifestation Lionel's jaw fell, more noisily than was its wont in moments of surprise.

His Aunt Saltfield turned, blushing. She took her hands away from the gentleman's and stood.

"I must tell you my news," Aunt Saltfield said. It seemed to Lionel that she actually looked thinner.

"Quickly, please, Aunt." He was attempting not to sound impolite. "There remains much to be done before the ceremony takes place."

"Of course, yes. I will be brief. You do remember Mr. Travit here, of course."

Now that he was impelled to consider this guest, Lionel nodded. The man was a journalist employed by one of the gossip organs.

"We've met." The only way to speed up the revelation was to anticipate it. "Have the two of you decided upon an arrangement?"

"We have, Your Lordship," Mr. Travit said in tones that were clear and gentlemanly if not cultured to the last degree. "You may rest assured, sir, that we plan to marry."

Faustine Saltfield, her voice lower than Lionel generally heard it, said shyly, "Mr. Travit has been here with me during the night, and we made our plans rather than do other things."

His aunt seemed a little confused, and Lionel didn't ask how Mr. Travit had found his way into the house at all. It seemed hardly to matter. He was looking at the journalist with narrow-lidded eyes.

"Mr. Travit and I will be living elsewhere," Mrs. Saltfield said immediately, "and he will be discreet in dealing with our family matters in case of necessity. He has proven in the past, as you will doubtless recall, that he can be discreet."

It was certainly so. Mr. Travit had attempted to enjoin a seemly silence upon at least one rival journalist after Miranda's status was publicly revealed at the Crystal Palace. Some courtesy had been earned by him as a result.

"Please excuse my preoccupation, Mr. Travit," he said, "and permit me to congratulate you upon the forthcoming nuptials."

"Thank you, sir."

Lionel extended a hand, and it was shaken vigorously. His

duty done, he proceeded up the stairs, not in any mood whatever to deal with the affianced happiness of others.

He could not have been aware of the thoughts that passed through Mr. Travit's mind and which, of course, the latter did not hesitate to share with the lady to whom he had just linked his future. If Wingham did indeed marry Miss Miranda Powell, it would offer a perfect opportunity for Travit to assure his rival, Mr. Cecil Hebden of *Day's Deeds,* that Miss Powell had been wed to Mr. Badger. As one result, every other newspaper but his own would be incorrect in its reporting.

Mr. Travit and his affianced chuckled as one over the prospect.

In a morning of surprising sights, the one which met Lionel's eyes upon entering the small sitting room of his home would forever deserve an honored place. For he encountered Charlotte Dempster in the arms of Oswald Badger and both in the throes of a kiss.

He had to cough two times before the pair detached themselves.

"The ground has indeed been cleared," Lionel said a little wryly to Mr. Badger, referring to the brief conversation downstairs shortly after they had entered.

Oswald Badger did not look embarrassed. "One thing led to another."

"Apparently it did. I am under the impression, my dear Charlotte, that a certain amount of news was communicated to you as well."

"Indeed it was," Miss Dempster agreed. "Dearest Oswald didn't intend any of it, yet, as he just said, one thing led to another."

Lionel noted mentally that she had never referred to him as "dearest" in the course of their commitment to marry. He felt no envy for Oswald Badger, only pleasure at having reached an understanding with the fine young woman before him.

"I am to infer, then, that it is Mr. Badger whom you love. Permit me to say that your choice will have my blessing."

"And yours with Miranda will be a cause of rejoicing for

myself and my dearest Oswald." Charlotte, suddenly thinking of a question, cocked her head so forcefully that her pale yellow glacé dress quivered, the gray sides shifting and the Irish-point black collar almost developing a fold. "You don't feel that the marriage you contemplate will offer additional food for scandal, Lionel, do you?"

"No." He had given it some thought, and a different decision would not have changed his mind about the path he would be following. "People may assume that I enjoyed myself with Miranda before the nuptials, but they will feel that by marrying I will have expiated my sins and be repenting for whatever previous pleasures had come to me."

Charlotte smiled. "You are pleased to be cynical."

"Only accurate, my dear Charlotte."

He was aware of Oswald Badger's strained smile. In this hour of his greatest happiness, Oswald was anticipating a future in which there would be little money between Charlotte and himself. He doubted, as Lionel did, that even the greatest happiness could long withstand a total lack of the blunt, such as faced them at this time.

There was a call from the other side of the door. "Charlotte, are you coming out?"

Lionel, like Charlotte herself, recognized the voice of Charlotte's mother. He guessed, too, that the murmuring on the other side of the door was caused by an intemperate discussion she was having with her husband. They seemed, this pair, the least possible endorsement for the married state. Long ago, however, Lionel had realized that the elder Dempsters actually enjoyed their bickering, that it was the form in which they communicated. From this it followed that a marriage could be defined as some legal arrangement which suited the two parties involved in it.

The door suddenly opened. Mr. Granville Dempster was heard saying, "In my opinion—"

"—which is worth little."

"In my opinion it was not one of my wiser investments."

"And so, of course, you purchased the stock shares."

"Only as a favor to Passy, who thinks he knows the Exchange

and will invest in any company with few shares available." He was recalling a discussion with the fabled Baron.

"Of course it was a good investment, contrary to what you think, or it wouldn't be offering a return."

"There is an only temporary favorable spurt in its progression, and I mean to sell now after the morning's news. Any firm which offers a product to turn base metals into gold would certainly attract the Baron, but cannot have the least staying power."

"Well, it must be better than your other foolish investments or it wouldn't be worth money, now."

"My other investments are excellent. The printing telegraph will be worth much money as soon as it is perfected, and the converter for making steel will be worth considerable, too, when the time comes."

"Those other things are worthless dreams and will never earn a farthing if they haven't done so after all this time."

Mr. Dempster's face turned a shade of deep red.

Charlotte was saying calmly but persistently, "I will join you both after only a few more moments."

Mrs. Dempster looked around and smiled at Lionel, who she felt certain was still her daughter's affianced. "I have no wish to interrupt any confabulation, to be sure. Come, Granville, and spare me your analysis of the gambling you have done on the so-called Exchange."

The door was closed on the angry Mr. Dempster.

Lionel said, "Your father is right, Charlotte, about one point. He may have gambled—a term I agree with—more money than was wise at the time, but progress in science is inevitable. When his other investments of which I have just heard begin to pay a return, and it may happen very shortly, he will reclaim the wealth he lost and far more."

"In which case," Charlotte said, for she was quick of intellect and immediately perceived the point her childhood friend was making, "there is no cause whatever to hesitate before following my heart."

"Exactly." Lionel observed once again that Mr. Badger's face remained a study in conflicting emotions. No doubt he could imagine the Dempsters' justifiable unhappiness with a young man of no income whatever. The idea that had briefly come to Lionel back in the cart a while ago, only to be forgotten because of the press of turbulent events, was once more present. In part, the words spoken by the intrusive Dempsters had recalled that concept to him.

Charlotte was saying, "My dearest Oswald and I will descend and notify the Reverend Mr. Gateshead of the change in the bridegroom's identity. Such matters as the banns not having been posted will offer no difficulty, Lionel, in light of your position in society. And, I might add, my dearest Oswald's powers of persuasion as well."

"I am aware of your affianced's persuasiveness." Lionel touched a newly tender place on his chin, where he had been struck after Oswald's behavior impelled him into battle. "Possibly I can now be of assistance to you two. Badger, you will need to earn an income in order to keep your own amour propre intact. Now, I ask myself, what skills do you have besides the persuasiveness of which Charlotte speaks?"

"I appreciate your kindness, but I fear I am not only lazy but a convincing liar when I wish to be. Those are not skills."

"Certainly they are if you choose a career in diplomatic negotiation," Lionel said, smiling. "Upon my restoration to the Elgin Commission, which must happen very shortly now if information coming to me can be accepted at its face value, I will make it my concern to require an assistant. It will offer a beginning to you, and you will in turn need the income to be gained from such futile endeavors."

The moment's silence that followed was caused by the others paying awed tribute to this stroke of combined genius and generosity.

"Lionel, you *are* a dear," Charlotte said, confirming the character she had previously assigned him.

The dear, however, was still facing Oswald. "But you must stay sober."

"I shall have no reason to drink intemperately from now on," Oswald said sincerely.

"You will when you learn about doings in the farthest reaches of diplomacy," Lionel countered. "I can but hope that you resist it."

"Depend upon me."

Lionel's curiosity was briefly aroused when he smiled encouragingly at Charlotte. He looked directly into her eyes in hopes of seeing the tawny flecks that Oswald had described with such admiration. Nothing of the sort presented itself to his inspection. Either he was shortsighted, which was doubtful, or he had never looked at Miss Dempster with the warmth of true love. The last notion confirmed an idea which had been borne upon him only recently.

"Ah, is Miranda in her room at this time?"

"To the very best of my knowledge," Charlotte said confidently, not revealing that Miranda had stayed overnight at the Ibbetson with her and the family and that all four had come to Jermyn Street together early this morning.

Without another word, for his felicitations had already been conveyed and he was absorbed by the prospect of embracing Miranda again, Lionel turned and left. He nodded briefly at the elder Dempsters, who awaited their daughter at the far end of the hall.

Left to themselves in the room, Charlotte looked away and started to the door. She didn't want to find herself delayed at this time by a romantic interlude.

Oswald, however, was standing before the dark-painted knob.

"A while ago, my lovely Charlotte, you described to me just how an ideal proposal of marriage ought to be made."

"Not at this time, dearest."

"I would normally agree, but I haven't proposed in so many words as yet and if I don't manage it now, I never will. Ahem! You suggested it be done by moonlight, a condition I cannot satisfy in the early afternoon."

"Permit me, then, to acknowledge the thought for the deed," Charlotte smiled.

"And you suggested it be done during a walk, which is a condition that I can indeed satisfy." Taking Charlotte's arm, he walked with her around the room. Charlotte chuckled irre-pressibly.

"Then, as I remember you saying, a male should turn the woman to face him." Lightly he drew Charlotte around. "With so much accomplished in his plan of campaign, he should look deeply into her eyes."

This he did, too, almost losing the thread of his discourse.

"He is now to speak in a thrilling voice," Oswald resumed at long last, abandoning the attempt to do so as he found himself suddenly hoarse. "Charlotte, dearest Charlotte, will you marry me?"

"Certainly, you scaramouche, my dearest scaramouche." Charlotte smiled.

She raised herself to kiss him as his head was descending toward hers. They were involved accordingly when a knock sounded at the door.

"I shall let my parents in," Charlotte said, separating herself reluctantly from her own true love. "There is much to tell them."

Oswald braced himself for a lively discussion which would bring all his own talents at reconciling opposition into the fullest play. He knew, though, even as Charlotte opened the door, that the matter would be settled exactly in the form that the two of them favored.

In this supposition he was shortly proved correct.

CHAPTER TWENTY-THREE

In Which
a Happy Ending
Is Produced in Time

Miranda sat wearily on her bed. She had endured much, spending the night with the bickering elder Dempsters in earshot and involved in truly frenzied discussions later on while the carriage ride to Jermyn Street was under way.

She had endured almost as much upon coming back. Mrs. Saltfield and a gentleman friend were so absorbed in each other that the former hardly spoke with Miranda. If the latter hadn't been certain that a woman of Mrs. Saltfield's age would not be so outrageous in aspect as to experience feelings of affection for a stranger, she would have assumed immediately that it was happening at this time. Miranda's imagination, always accepting the worst, made it seem only too possible.

News that she found even more appalling was yet to come. It soon developed that Lionel hadn't yet returned home. Visions of her beloved being killed or gravely wounded flared before her, as vivid as that odious wallpaper with which her eyes had been afflicted upon arriving at this house.

As a consequence, she jumped up in fright when a series of gentle knocks sounded against the panel. Her first thought was simply that news of Lionel's extreme condition was being brought to her.

The door opened on the Earl himself, who stepped into the room but wisely kept the door open.

"Lovely," he said at the sight of her.

Miranda, in the embellished blond lace bridal gown, disregarded the compliment and rushed forward. She had already observed the discoloration on Lionel's face and the rumpled condition of his rig-out.

"What foul thing has happened to you?"

"Nothing in the least serious," he said. "Everything is well."

"*You* aren't."

"I can assure you that I have rarely felt better. Already I have been in extensive discussions with Charlotte, and we have reached a modus vivendi."

It fled Miranda's mind that she had wanted to tell Lionel with light mockery that she had been the one to first inform Charlotte last night about the changed circumstances among the three of them.

"And you were hurt by Oswald, I'll be bound!"

"Not at all, dear. The damage to me took place before my seeing Charlotte."

"You were lured into some foul establishment and set upon by brigands."

"In a sense I was lured and certainly I was set upon, but only after I had established that a state of hostility existed between myself and those who successfully defended themselves."

"Oswald lured others to attack you," she stormed. "He is a low hound, and I shall tell him so as soon as might be."

"That isn't quite correct, either, and I may point out that it hardly poses an important issue for us at this particular time."

"What happened?" Miranda was finding it difficult to control the highest flights of an ever-soaring imagination. "You must tell me exactly what happened, the worst of it."

"Oswald was drinking in a solitary way, and then he hurled himself upon another man, intending to save that other from what looked to him like an effort at self-destruction but was only an attempt to entertain the patrons in hopes of raising some money for himself."

"I am more confused by this explanation than I would have believed was humanly possible," Miranda confessed, briefly distracted from the conviction that Lionel had been in discourse with the devil incarnate.

"It is quite simple," Lionel said, his patience beginning to fray. "The entertainer had taken a lighted taper and placed it into his mouth, proving that he could swallow fire. Myself, I believe that some trickery is involved in so doing, but that is beside the point."

Miranda's eyes widened. Her theory about the presence of the devil had apparently been confirmed.

"I can tell you that Oswald generously attempted to remove the taper from that entertainer's mouth, whereupon the latter's colleague reacted adversely. When I tried to redress the balance, as both men had joined in an assault upon Oswald, I was set upon."

"And hurt! Don't forget that you were badly hurt."

"Not badly at all, I can assure you." He laughed at the excessive concern she was showing. Miranda imagined that he was hiding the pain he must have felt at that gesture. To herself she approved of his bravery although certain she was seeing through it.

"Nevertheless, you must immediately go to your room, Lionel, and rest."

"By no means." He was only smiling this time. "I plan to go downstairs and be married."

"You don't mean married to—?" The worst had once again occurred to her.

"Of course not. Charlotte and Oswald are determined to wed each other, and Oswald is to become an assistant to me in my conscientious pursuit of European harmony on Britain's terms."

Miranda was fond of Oswald, to be sure, but couldn't help visualizing a continent torn apart by strife as a result of his peacemaking efforts.

"Nonetheless, you need to rest, Lionel."

He shook his head firmly. "What I need is to marry you, preferably right away."

She suddenly recalled that not even her older sister had been invited to the wedding planned for herself and Oswald Badger. It was an omission she would have liked to redress, but saw no opportunity if Lionel persisted. No doubt she would be forgiven, but further attempts ought to be made on her older sister's behalf.

"The reverend will protest if it is you who marries me," she pointed out weakly.

"Not for long. Charlotte has gone down to soothe him and her gentleness, allied to Oswald's one-man-to-another manner and the knowledge of my rank, should still the reverend gentleman's reservations."

"But you—you aren't dressed!"

"Only a few touches are needed here and there," said the Earl, wiping dust flecks off his trousers and jacket. "Now I am as fit for the proceedings as ever I will be." He looked concerned. "You do want to marry me, Miranda, isn't that so?"

From the small sitting room she could hear a sudden explosion of angry conversation, which she readily accepted as issuing from Mr. and Mrs. Dempster. In her eyes they were a sad pair, and she could not imagine such unhappiness following a link between herself and a warm and restrained and practical yet imaginative man like the Earl of Wingham. She wanted nothing more than to assay a marriage of her own, and particularly with this man who was determined to marry her.

"Yes, I want to," she said sincerely. "Of course I want to."

"Then I can foresee no further obstacle to our doing so."

"Only one," she said, and this time she sounded unwilling to proceed.

"What would that be?"

"You might suffer a further onset of weakness, a relapse."

"I can assure you once again that there is no danger whatever of any such happening."

"Certainly you would say so, but that doesn't mean such a dreadful event might not occur."

"I assure you that I am fully capable of going downstairs before you do and waiting until you and your party see fit to arrive at the altar. Presumably Oswald will serve as my best man. When it comes time to say 'I do,' I assure you that I will be able to speak in robust tones."

"I cannot dispute that much any longer, considering how well you sound."

"Then we have finally arrived at an agreement."

"Something else has occurred to me," Miranda confessed.

"I felt a lurking suspicion that it would," his lordship confessed. "Tell me what it is and most likely that particular bogey can be dispelled, too."

"I wondered what might happen afterwards," Miranda said, looking down modestly.

For once, Lionel misunderstood her. "At the wedding meal, you mean? I can fully withstand the rigors of feeding myself. Friends will be nearby and congratulating me upon my good judgment whilst hiding their envy."

"No, I didn't mean that, either."

"Well, once the feeding has been accomplished and guests leave, Miranda, the two of us will be alone." He looked astonished. "Can *that* be what you mean, Miranda?"

"I felt that as you have experienced some weakness already, it might recur and interfere with the fullest possible enjoyment of this occasion."

"I see," Lionel said truthfully, astonished and yet pleased. "There is nothing to be said about that. I will be fit or not. The only way to find out is to take the risk."

"But wouldn't you rather put it off until we can be certain all will be well?"

"There can be no certainty along that line or any other, my dear," he said softly. "One can only accept what is called the balance of probabilities. On the evidence of my current fitness and anticipation it is reasonable to say that I will be in the best of shape for what is to occur soon enough. Further than that, I cannot say, and neither could any other human being."

There was truth in his words. The quest for perpetual certainty, taking form in the attempt to visualize every possible horrid eventuality and protect herself against it, was doomed to failure. She could only live from day to day, doing the best she was able and using such good common sense as had been granted to her.

"And when you see how fit I am," Lionel added, "when you 038 know full well how very fit I am, I shall remind you of this occasion in the future as soon as you start imagining calamities that could never occur."

She smiled and came into his arms.

Mrs. Jossy, the generous but unsmiling housekeeper, had made her way upstairs to determine politely what was holding up the appearance of the groom. A footman, keeping at a discreet distance, accompanied her.

Mr. Badger and Miss Dempster were discovered together in the small sitting room, arm in arm and smiling with great affection at each other.

Mrs. Jossy fled down the hall and came to Miss Miranda Powell's door. It was partway open. An unavoidable look inside showed the lovely Miss Powell in the arms of his lordship. It seemed precisely fitting, and a far more satisfactory pairing, in both cases, than had previously been planned.

For the first time in the knowledge of anyone in this establishment, Mrs. Jossy gave a hearty laugh.

The footman saw and heard, but the Earl and Miss Miranda weren't at all affected by what was taking place so near to them. The groom and bride-to-be had eyes only for each other and ears for nothing at all.